DOWN THE HUME

DOWN THE HUME

DOWN THE HUME
PETER POLITES

hachette
AUSTRALIA

hachette
AUSTRALIA

Published in Australia and New Zealand in 2017
by Hachette Australia
(an imprint of Hachette Australia Pty Limited)
Level 17, 207 Kent Street, Sydney NSW 2000
www.hachette.com.au

10 9 8 7 6 5 4 3 2 1

National Library of Australia
Cataloguing-in-Publication data

Polites, Peter, author.
Down the hume/Peter Polites.

ISBN: 978 0 7336 3556 4 (pbk)

Noir fiction, Australian.

A823.4

Cover design by Grace West
Cover image courtesy Stocksy.com
Author photograph courtesy Stelios Papadakis
Text design by Bookhouse, Sydney
Typeset in 12.5/18 pt Garamond Premier Pro
Printed and bound in Australia by McPherson's Printing Group

Before the sun got up I had morning dreams filled with screaming babies; when I woke it was just the cats fucking outside my bedroom window. I opened the window, took a deep breath of fresh air, but all I smelled was shit and cat sex.

I'd wake up all 'up and at 'em!' then – you know – I'd step into the kitchen and the cockatiel would sing at me. I wanted to run up to its cage and scream at the yellow and grey thing, 'Die, you demon bird! You should be extinct like your brothers the dinosaurs!' but there was no point.

When I went into the kitchen, I would find uncooked oats on the bench. There was also a barrel of banana-flavoured Muscle Milk Protein with no lid on it and a scoop next to it; the powder would be everywhere, on the laminate, on the steak knives, on the kettle.

Nice Arms Pete was hardly there in the mornings. At the time he was my boyfriend, though sometimes I thought he was my roommate. Or maybe I was his fucktoy, his sidepiece. He spent more time at the gym than at home. At the time I forgave him for this. Because of the way his traps fell out of his singlet, or how his biceps were two throbbing white mounds.

How did I get there?

Θεός προσέχομαι. I got there after some accidents.

When I was a kid I walked to school alone and got the evil eye placed on me by a creep. Now a white windowless van follows me everywhere. Even now when I meet new babies and cats, I wonder if they see what is under the scars that run across my cheek.

My life wasn't any good at home. Mama was mousy and beaten, compensated with psychic reachouts. Made moolah reading coffee cups and spent hundreds on fortune tellers. Old women or men in the καφενία with grey beards and a deck of cards. She worried in tears and dreams were a go-to, where she talked with departed men. Eventually her dreams filled with a son cast out because he didn't want to shatter disco balls.

To her, I was before after everyone. Once she woke up in matted bed sheets seeing my thin legs running through a castle made of chemicals in glass tubes. That same morning, she looked out the bedroom window and saw a fleet of black cockatoos picking the seeds of a pine. The breath fled from her body.

'Δεν θέλω πουστις σε τούτο σπίτι,' said Baba. An angry wall of Baba post 'The Coming Out' meant my rebellion shoplift, arrest and drug phase. Yeah, cringe-worthy cliché. What's really unfortunate is that clichés ring true.

I held down assistant nursing jobs. Got fired for fighting. Got fired for cutting an enemy's tyres. Worked at a bowlo, met Nice Arms Pete, didn't know it but that's when my troubles really started.

Went back to aged care. Lifting oldies, twisting my lower spine, changing brown and yellow stained sheets in the middle of the burbs. Nice Arms Pete and I moved in together and I tried harder than him to make it work.

I shouldn't be held ransom to sienna roofs and red, yellow, green wheelie bins. This place, it's purgatory, it's shit. Back to where I came from? Nah, not there. Those mountains are just stories now where ex-landowning peasants direct a confession to God and saints and Παναγιότα herself. As their eyes cloud with cataracts they sing in unison from their nursing home beds: Εχουμε γεραση στην ξενιτία. We have become old in a foreign land. But there are enough people like me here that have the same flags in common.

I dressed for work in blue scrubs, packed things in my yellow bag. I'd lock the front door, walk halfway down the street then walk back to check that it was locked. I would do that three times. Then I'd cross myself. Πατερ Ημών.

First. Can I just say? About all this. Nice Arms Pete is the human equivalent of a trigger warning. Which meant that I was the one who was loaded. Bang, ready to go off.

AUBURN ROAD

That day I did good. I got outta work early, rode the bus home. The 119 slithered through the industrial area. An invisible dome separated red roofs from factories, child care centres from brothels. Every second business had a For Rent sign out front. Every second warehouse was shutting down.

Outside the bus window hi-vis lumpens speckled the streets, sultanas in a fruit loaf. Takeaways sold dollar-something bacon and egg rolls and cappuccino meal deals. The bus stopped two or three times. Each stop more men wearing bright yellow shirts and blue canvas pants got on.

Then, a random hottie. Had the work-a-day bright orange shirt on, blue denim thick around his legs.

A Benny Barba fade, number one clippers with a Nile River part, pomade slick. Mixed-race footy body from the Pacifica to Cape Town. Watched him stomp steel-capped boots down the bus, pulling at his half tucked-in shirt, looking like a donkey pretending to be a show horse. There's not much difference between being a man and being a horse, except they shoot horses, don't they? As Horseboy walked past I felt the heat radiate off him. Felt the heat on parts of my arm that I broke when I was a kid.

That Horseboy, he got at me. But Nice Arms Pete was an infection in my head. Nice Arms Pete with two little fluoride canines that jutted in front of messed-up teeth. Stuck right into the parts of my head that had pictures of red roofs and Colorbond fences. Nice Arms Pete who should've been waiting for me at the cottage we rented together.

When I first met him I told him what my name was in Greek. He got the accents on top of the vowels right. Rolled his R's like a Greek when he said 'Lambrraki'.

'Why does everyone call you Bux?' he asked. 'Why doesn't everyone call you Lamb?'

I explained it to him. The diminutive of Lambros is Lambraki; people started calling me Baki and in primary school a little blond boy who came from Queensland shortened it to Bux. But Nice Arms Pete never called me Bux. After saying my Greek name correctly once he never used that again either. He would always say, 'Baby, can you get the pizza from out front?' or, 'Baby, stop going through my phone' or even, 'Hey you, come here.'

My stop was just inside the industrial area. I danced around a herd of hi-vis gorillas who stood in the aisle of the bus. Couldn't help it. Did an up-downer to Horseboy before getting off the bus. That little bugalugs had butter-scotch biceps and blunt eyes. Made my dick twitch.

The cottage we rented bordered train tracks on one side and a soccer field on the other. As I walked over the bridge, a train went under my feet. The metal bones of the bridge shook and I could see early winter condensa-tion forming around the soccer fields. Trees around the side of the park were blurry. Beyond the trees, normal suburbia. A kilometre away was Greenacre. Kids rode bikes without helmets and cousins sprayed bullets into each other's houses.

Noticed this pair of headlights travelling down along the field. The glowing eyes made their way towards me. As I reached the front of the house so did they. A Hell Red Commodore. It was smooth and shiny, the bonnet had a scoop. Tinted black windows meant I couldn't see inside. The passenger door opened. Two long denim legs came out and Nice Arms Pete flicked popcorn-blond hair out of his eyes. Saw me staring at him. My mouth dropped. Took quick breaths. Nice Arms Pete turned to the driver and mouthed something, then got out. The Hell Red Commodore sped off. Nice Arms Pete stood there facing me.

'Pardon me, but your husband is showing,' I said, tapping my chest. Nice Arms Pete walked towards me. His Nike Shox had a Richter scale that sensed my anger. Placed two massive palms on my shoulders. The fingers reached all around each muscle, anchored me to him. He sighed. 'Work opportunity, making a few wickets.'

I leaned into him. Nice Arms Pete was taller than me and my head fell between his neck and shoulders. He smelled like pot-smoke musk, fabric softener and sweat. The streetlamp overhead made a tent of light.

We opened the gate, walked to the door. Nice Arms Pete had planted bushes that sprouted pretty full, already they hid the front of the house. The cottage, like most Sydney developments, was a joke. Used to be a one-room shack, raised high on bricks. First room had a queen mattress and built-in wardrobes made from plywood, a curved mirror that distorted how I saw myself. Sometime in the history of the house a second room was added, lower to the ground but higher ceilings than the first. This was the living room. In there we had an electricity-guzzling plasma that usually hummed static. The grey light lit up a second-hand couch and some unpacked boxes. The next room added was a kitchen and an eating space, with a laundry and a bathroom attached. Walls were painted omelette yellow and had black-and-white chequerboard tiles. To access each room, we had to walk through the rooms preceding it. It was a maze. With limited exits. A backyard with patches of concrete and my attempt at food gardening. Planter boxes with dead tomato plants.

I held the door open for him. Nice Arms Pete breezed through the bedroom to the living room and fell onto the couch. 'All this stuff, can we get rid of it?' he called out to me. He meant the unpacked boxes, full of porcelain figurines. I was in the bedroom changing out of my scrubs into grey marle sweats.

'Let me go through it first. Stuff I want to keep,' I said as I picked up dirty clothes from the bedroom floor. I glanced into the living room.

Nice Arms Pete was using a key to slice into the masking tape sealing a box. He spread the cardboard flaps, pulled out an ancient Greek drama mask. It had a startled ceramic face. The mouth on it formed a perfect round hole, looked like it was yelling or shocked. Anguish eyes. Long messy hair framing a matt white face.

'WTF?' said Nice Arms Pete. He held up the mask and interpreted it. 'Been around, this mask,' he said.

'Our people have them. Every home I been in has 'em. Cheap trinkets for tourists. Let it go, yeah.'

The mask used to sit on a wall, under a photograph of my parents in front of the Acropolis – a photograph that all Greek families have. In my folks' home there was a wall dedicated to the ancients. A Greek fantasy that we were among white marble temples and the beginnings of democracy, walking around in flowing white sheets with wreaths of olive leaves around our heads.

When Baba left periodically the wall changed. The shrine would be framed by empty longnecks of VB; they went all the way up the hallway. My tiny feet couldn't negotiate the obstacle course of the empty brown bottles. Mama would be passed out on top of the bed. The neatly made bed, with its dark green cover and polyester blankets, sharp like a paper stack. Long messy hair framed her face. Her eyes loosely shut. Her mouth open, that same perfect circle.

'This shit . . .' Nice Arms Pete rotated the mask in his hands, 'it opens a shed door to your weakness, bro.' He put it over his face, biceps bulging. I looked at my partner's face covered with this mask of anguish, large pec muscles like plates bursting out of his singlet. I lost my balance and fell backwards, landed on the mattress.

'You in a mask and just a big white body is totally working for me ATM,' I said to him, lying on the bed.

Got up. Went to the kitchen. I held the fridge door open with one arm, leaned into the cold. Three brown bottles of VB, one head of broccoli and a plastic container. Nice Arms Pete wandered in from the living room.

'And the cupboard was bare . . . No groceries today?' I said.

Nice Arms Pete put the mask on the counter top, moved around me and stole a bottle of beer out of the fridge. Twisted the sharp metal in his hand. Angled the bottle, poured the liquid into small plastic cups. I closed the fridge door, turned around and rested on it. Nice Arms Pete offered me a beer, apologising for not getting any groceries.

'You said you were all future and no past when we met.' I took the drink from him.

'That's why I don't keep those things.' Nice Arms Pete pointed to the mask on the counter, walked towards me, angled his body into me. 'Don't you want that too?' he said.

Nice Arms Pete sculled the rest of the beer. Head tilted back, throat muscles contracting rhythmically. My eyes looked at Nice Arms Pete's rockmelon arse, then to the counter where the bottle sat next to the faux ancient mask.

'If we are all future and no past then who was in that car that dropped you off?'

'He wants me to move stuff. For money. He is a boy,' said Nice Arms Pete. He was facing away from me, his small waist and back sprouting like a muscular fountain.

'Boys have a strange way of becoming men.'

'He looks like a man. Bit woggy-looking too. Yeah but nah.' Shook his head at the end, eyes went somewhere casual, blowing it away.

'Seriously, a wog?'

'Don't trust me, eh? You wanna go through my phone?' Nice Arms Pete pulled out his smartphone. Thrust it in front of my face. I could look everywhere apart from the phone and my partner. Nice Arms Pete, cheeks flushed. Blue veins on his neck throbbed. Clicked it in him. He repeated, 'Here!' louder, louder. I swatted the hand away. 'You'll go through it anyway. Here, take it.' Pegged the phone at my head. I ducked. Bounced off the wall and landed on the chequerboard floor. The phone broke into three parts: battery, case and body.

Outside the cottage, a train on tracks zoomed. Echoed all through the mist-filled backyard.

'I'm sure lots of random hot wogs just want to give you a job.' Said it to him as I was bending over to pick up the pieces of the smartphone.

'He's a roid muncher, a gym queen, a juicehead with bacne. Gonna move Dyna Bolts for him. Nothing spesh, easy money,' said Nice Arms Pete.

I stood up, handed him the phone, my hairy arm extended. I looked at the ivory of Nice Arms Pete's forearm with milk jelly smooth muscle and marbled veins.

'You are using roids, aren't ya?'

'How can I sell if I don't know how they work?' said Nice Arms Pete. It was a hiss, spit landed on my chin.

'How can you sell it if you don't fuck him?' I just said it, my eyes scanned the surface of Nice Arms Pete's face. It was slowly contorting and puffing up with red. Tops of his eyelids creasing, lips slamming against each other.

His fist shot out. Struck the side of my face. Nostrils got pushed down, my neck clenched taking the blow, and my eyes expanded post impact. I spun around away from him, put my whole arm on the wall and slumped into my body. I held up the walls with my arm, because if I didn't the whole house would have crashed. I breathed into my lungs but the worry beads spun around in a tornado.

Nice Arms Pete hotfooted it. Heard him push over the empty beer bottle; it rolled off the counter and broke on the floor. In the living room I heard the bulb shatter as the lamp fell over. In the bedroom he knocked over a chair, made a thud on the wooden floors. Heard him fling open the front door, the door hitting the plasterboard.

I ran to the bedroom. There was a hole in the plasterboard from where the knob pushed in. Saw him just beyond the fence as he walked into the park.

Condensation from the grass and the cold air created an envelope of mist around his shape.

The arm that I broke as a kid tingled.

I ran after him. Caught up in the middle of the soccer field.

Nice Arms Pete kept walking. He walked from the middle to the goals. I heard the sounds my feet made flattening blades of moist grass. Kept following him. At the goals he turned around. Skin so white, face visible in the dark.

Reached up, placed my hand on his shoulder.

'I should have known better,' I said.

He touched my face. When his hand went along my bruised top lip and my almost broken nose, I winced from the pain. His fist went into a deep denim pocket. Pulled out a Syrinapx bottle, twisted the cap off and handed me two light blue pills.

I stood opposite Nice Arms Pete. The two little moons shone in my olive hands. Streetlight filtered through the trees casting a frame of shadows around the soccer field. We stood in the net.

PARK ROAD

Everyone called it Sydney winter but WTF. Bright cold yellow-blue skies. Blinds weren't a barrier to that annoying morning light. The sun woke me early and set the tone. Wrecked. Sleepless. Never refreshed. But oh! The Syrinapx! It took the sheen off the sun and dulled its glare; my eyes had in-built polarised lenses.

My bed was empty. I got dressed in scrubs, noticed Nice Arms Pete's Nike Shox weren't in their spot. Led to those shallow quick breaths. Front part of my brain became really hot.

I used bed sheets for curtains. My fingers released the pegs that clipped them to the window frame. The sheets fell to the floor. That Sydney winter sun came in and filled up the room. Oblong dust balls cast shadows like mini chocolate Easter eggs.

Took my shopping bag and left the cottage. At the bus stop I smoked Fine Cut Whites. Waited for a bus that would cut through the industrial area to my workplace, Park Road Aged Care.

The home was in the shape of an L. Admin and supplies were in the bottom of the L, residents' rooms, recreation space up the spine.

When I started my shift, I didn't even look at who was on reception. Took off my jumper in the staff admin office, put it in my bag. Turned off my phone. Logged number onto work. 6661. Put bag away in the locker.

A door on either side of the room. One general supplies: antibacterial cleaning products, backpack vacuums, sterile bins, wipes, sponges. Powder-coated gloves. The other a meds supply closet: smaller, locked, tablets and bottles neatly lined up. There was a change room and shower next door.

We had a series of rotating doctors doing check-ups.

Typical kind of mixed bag socially retarded doctor types, the kinds that were born into med school. Asian chicks that could be regulation hot but instead wore Asics everywhere. Young Viet dudes making their fugee parents proud with their God complex. Muscle Indian gay boy doctors who spoke with phony deep voices. Persian hotties who emerged from north of the bridge and had nothing to do with any of the local Iranians.

Tucked in my scrubs before starting work. With one hand I pulled at the front of my pants and with the other pushed my shirt deep past the drawstrings. Every time I did that, it reminded me of being a puppy and my mama fixing me up. She would take the bottom of the collared blue shirt in her hand and pull out the elastic grey shorts I was wearing. Her hands would push the front of my shirt deep into my shorts and pull the waistline to the bellybutton. 'Now I am making you handsome,' she would say. She kept doing this till I was in my teens; eventually I had to push her away.

When I was in the admin office the head nurse walked in. Tall. Garish. Cigarette skin. Copper Spanish Filo. Agatha cracked a smile, lips too tight together. She nodded. Made a line for the meds room. Penrith panther to a hiding spot.

'Hello, Bux, how are you doing today?' Vowels inflected, her accent a Filomerican drawl.

From a stainless-steel yoyo attached to her hip she pulled on her plastic swipe, extending it in front of her. A barrier against me.

'Oh . . . I'm, er . . . had some probs,' I said in one breath.

Agatha let the swipe retract into her body.

I was about to continue but she interrupted.

'Let's talk about it later, Bux. One-on-one, make sure your morning duties are completed.' She spoke in a neutral tone but that Filomerican accent was too singsong – seemed like there was a hint of a smile. She extended the electronic tag from her yoyo again. Made her way to the meds closet. Right arm swiped on the pad and her left hand opened the door. As Agatha disappeared into the closet, I looked at the treasures through the open door.

I reckon the repetition of the rows of pill bottles hypnotised me.

Started morning duties.

Task number one: get all the mobile patients into the recreation room. Some of the residents needed a push out of bed, then they used the walker to go to the recreation room. Others had to be slid onto wheelchairs and then rolled down the hallway. Had twelve patients to work through; the other eighteen stayed in bed.

Bruno was my favourite patient. Bruno didn't yell, swear or throw his faeces.

Shifted four other geris in Bruno's room first. Moved them down the hall to the recreation room. They had names that you just don't hear anymore. Vera, Pasquale, Pauletta, Aida. For some reason they put most of the old Italians in Bruno's room. Usually they all got along, but Vera and Pasquale were northerners. I used to tease them, say stuff like, 'Hey! Polentini! You are more Swedish than Italian.' That would shit them. Vera would yell at me, 'We are Italian!', gesturing with her fists, while the others turned down their hearing aids. 'The southerners are Arabs! Dirty moors!'

I went to Bruno, pulled back the sheet, exposing his legs.

'Bux, you got girlfriend yet?'

Residents invaded me with questions around girlfriends, marriage and kids. Straight acting fatigue. Old people have envy eyes over my frame, my clear olive skin.

I lifted Bruno's legs to move them onto the wheelchair, the tendons of his ankles visible beneath the skin.

'No, Bruno. No girlfriend.'

There was a faded colour photograph on Bruno's nightstand. The frame of the photograph was hard metal; you could tell it was made in a time when even cheap things were made to last. The photo was of a younger Bruno and another guy. In the picture Bruno was reclining on the dunes of a beach, short black swimmers, high-waisted, tight around his crotch and thighs. The other man had curly blond hair, a solid body; he wore looser shorts that weren't made for swimming but they were wet. A cigarette dangled from the blond man's mouth. His body was terse, his muscle definition was the kind that crazed me. Bruno's face was on the cusp of a riot. I thought that the old photo looked like an Instagram.

'Please exercise legs, please exercise my legs.'

'I'm not supposed to.' I went to the side of the bed and lifted Bruno's foot. It was lukewarm; varicose veins cased it like a protective layer. My hand moved up to hold his inner thigh so that he would be able to move his legs better. I moved the foot towards Bruno's head making the knee bend, then repeated the action.

'I used to run for family,' said Bruno. 'I used to run and get cigarettes, run to get the mail, I used to run to get the ferry.' A sigh exited his body. Thin chest weak from smoking. Mediterranean skin now all polluted.

'Bruno, tell me the story of the photo again?'

Just then two of the cleaners came in to start on the room. I told them to come back later.

'You know what life is? Life isn't this.' He gestured to the room around him. Struck his hand into the passionless air. 'Life isn't clean floors!' Flicked his wrist to the floor, speckled light blue linoleum. Grabbed at the sheets on the bed, white. 'Life isn't dry-cleaned sheets!'

The ceiling was painted inoffensive pink and the odour of the residents had been sanitised out. Constant temperature in the room, never varied. While I exercised Bruno's legs a scent of sweat wafted from my underarms, fell into Bruno's hairy nostrils. Bruno shut his eyes and recited: 'You miss sweat. You miss the stink of a bath-room. You miss the smell of humans. You miss the smell of shit.'

'I don't. Dot in the other room threw her shit at me. It missed. Landed on the vegetable opposite.'

'Aha. She's an old cunt, that one.' Bruno breathed it out.

I zipped my mouth and threw away the key.

'I used to say that to my wife: "You are an old cunt." And she would say to me: "When will you die, you old cock?" I wish I never got married.' Bruno tried to look towards the nightstand, but his eyes were facing ahead and he couldn't see the picture in the frame. Heard this quiver in his voice.

'Bruno, tell me about the picture again.' Hoping to distract him. I asked him while looking at his legs, moving his feet backwards and forwards, making sure I got the bend in.

'I was a young man once and those days were a long time ago.' Bruno's eyes rested on the ceiling. He was about to cry.

I finished extending and retracting one leg. Moved around the bed to work the other leg. Picked up Bruno's milky blue foot.

'Well . . . Let me tell about him . . .' Bruno said, and once again was interrupted.

From behind me I heard Agatha's accent and her austere directions. She spoke to me in a monotone in front of the patients.

'Bux, I told you not to do that.' There was a sternness in Agatha's voice. It was louder too, booming across the room.

I stopped what I was doing and turned around to apologise. She cut me off.

'Put him in the chair and take him down the hallway,' she said.

I picked up both of Bruno's legs, moved them around to hang off the side of the bed. Bruno lifted himself from the rails and I eased him into the wheelchair.

'Bloody hell, mate,' said Bruno. His thick Italian accent gave way on the *mate*, said it like he was mimicking a drongo. 'In my country her people are cleaners. Not bosses. Not even allowed to bloody vote.'

Agatha heard everything.

From behind the wheelchair, I gave Agatha a shrug. Mouthed, 'Sorry.'

She dismissed it with a wave.

I wheeled Bruno down the hall. He started confessing, like it was a Sacrament of Penance and I was a priest. Spoke in a hushed tone through an imaginary latticework.

'He was an Australian. A really one, the kind I never be. Pete was his name. I thought to myself, "Is this a man?

Is this an Australian? Down at pub every day? Eating rubbish foods?" Pete didn't know how to eat when we came here, Pete didn't know how to clean and cook, he no know about war life.'

Black rubber wheels rolled across linoleum floor, almost louder than the hush-hush secret confession. We passed an empty room on one side. It reminded me of a fiery patient.

Bruno offered an opinion. 'You like me. But I am resigned, an old Venetian lion. Them and they, throw the poo, throw the shit, you should like them more, like the old men and women here who throw their shit at you, who spit at you, they have not resigned, they still raging.'

'So they are not throwing shit at me but dignity?'

'Ah ha ha ha.' Bruno swayed as he laughed.

I parked him in front of the plasma. On the television screen a blonde wig with teeth was excited about a vacuum cleaner. Bruno looked up at the screen, let out a sigh. 'Fuck this country,' he said.

Left Bruno in that room. Started next set of tasks. Went to supply room. Took trolley that had large yellow bag attached to it and bedding materials. Went around to the unoccupied beds.

There is dignity in doing a shit job well. I replaced plastic underlays, sheets, sprayed and wiped surfaces with HG-35 antibacterial spray. Used sheets went into the yellow bag for offsite cleaning. As the bag filled, I moved closer and closer to having a cigarette and coffee break. Travelled down the hall, room to room.

Task finished, went to staffroom. Turned on kettle. Got the Fine Cut Whites. Water boiled. Made cup of Nescafé. Went to smoking courtyard and found Agatha there. Mimed the gesture of a lighter with my hands.

'Don't steal it,' said Agatha. She handed me the lighter. 'This lighter is a boomerang.'

The courtyard was a small space accessed through a side door. Far from an actual courtyard. Staff would say, 'Courtyard ciggie fiver.' Or, 'Yarn and smoko courtyard.' What they meant was a small sucky space on the side of the building closed off by a fence.

'I'm sorry about doing Bruno's leg exercises.' I puffed on my cigarette mechanically; it decreased my anxiety.

Agatha's smile was terse.

'Sometimes my head isn't here.' A queer pause. 'I just moved in with someone,' I said.

'I put on a sheet of diamonds when I come to work,' said Agatha. She smoked rollies. Workday mornings rolled nine cigarettes. She would smoke them throughout the day and night. 'I mean, I imagine putting on a blanket of diamonds when I come to work and I leave everything else outside.' She held the cigarette in her two fingers and pointed it to the sky. Examined the ember glowing red, eyes up close, like the muted fire held her thoughts.

'Yeah. It's just that, I think I'm having some problems with him. You see, we broke up, got back together and decided to live together . . .'

Agatha extinguished her cigarette butt in the dirt of a pot plant. She tucked loose strands of hair behind her ears. Looked into my eyes, gave a smile with a tight mouth, patted me on the shoulder and left the courtyard.

CALDWELL PARADE

When I try to think about all the places where I have wage slaved, they become a series of shapes, colours and smells.

Just after high school, I worked at one of those we-have-it-all-at-a-discount department stores. It was a chain. There was a giant team. I spent Sundays coming down. Reading *Cleo* magazine behind the hardware paint counter and pashing on with another wog boy at the back of lay-by storage. He was the most femme Hercules I'd ever met in my life. His long lashes were like a siren call. So I'd sneak over to him when I was bored. He would be leaning on the counter, big eyes like a cow's and a hook nose. Flicking a pen in his hands the way cows munch on grass. 'What's up, big boy?' I'd ask, he'd look up, dull eyes, and I'd push him up against the shelves lined with tricycles. But if you ask me to remember the place, what it looked like, all I can think of is the colour blue, hard plastic signs and giant numbers printed to look like they were digital.

When I was trying to go to TAFE, I worked at a porno book store. We were in the middle period of Myspace and people had to endure using their legs to get porn on a VHS. Metrosexuals hadn't been swallowed up by the pornosexuals. The gen pop still had vestiges of shame around this vulgar erotica, but apart from embarrassed faces all I remember is yellow price tags and the pink of flesh images. If I think about it now, the only thing I can smell is the litres of hand sanitiser I used.

The old folks' home is a montage of pastel colours on hard materials. The neutral colour on the plasterboard of the hallway, the speckled linoleum of the floor, the metal of the beds. The residents – resis for short – they bled into the surfaces. Not literally. Actually, yes – sometimes literally. Like when a resi with thin blood scraped himself with a fork and the blood became a lake on the melamine table. 'Blood thinners!' cried the old man. 'Oh, these blood thinners!' And I wiped and sprayed and chucked out paper towels.

The place was part hospital, part asylum, part mortuary. Thirty residents. A few of them had Alzheimer's, some were just angry, others were straight-out nut bars. The ones with functioning bodies but dust minds – they got at me.

But there was this strange overlap in the place. That sanitised space became more and more infected with their personalities. Saw their hard-headed anger in the store-bought art that hung on walls. Found an old man's joy in an inconveniently placed fire extinguisher closet.

Working with old people is like smoking the bud of a hand-rolled cigarette. Everything slows because you move to their pace. Don't upset them with a quick drag; they might fall apart. You notice their millimetre hand tremors or how their limbs move at a languid tempo.

In the first month of working there, Fufu – she got at me too. She had a canvas body but the tone in her voice was a floral print.

'Call me Fufu, darling. My twenty grandchildren do,' she said. Spoke English with that French accent most of the freshie Lebs have here.

She was stout. Short hair cropped close, no grey. Would have been on the late side of eighty. Gave her this sweet energy. We bonded when we found out that we both started smoking cigarettes too young. Hands were cartoons and her eyes as animated as I was. She was bedridden the whole time that I was there. Never talked to me about the weather and never asked me about girlfriends. Refreshing.

Whenever she started remembering her dead husband, I could easily cheer her up. I reminded her about her house on Caldwell Parade. They'd bought it in the seventies, built it up into a palace, and she raised seven children there. I reminded her about the twenty grandchildren that existed because of her.

'Your job in life is done,' I would say to her. 'You have lived and laughed and loved everyone you can.'

Fufu said that I reminded her of a Greek man she'd worked for. She was a seamstress in a factory as soon as the oldest kids in her family were big enough to take care of the little ones. Spoke a few Greek words to impress me. Κούκλο. Καμάρι. Touched my cheek and called me 'darling' when I went close. Told me more and more about the Greek man that she'd worked for: Costa had my dark skin; apparently my sweetness and charisma too.

Never said to her that she reminded me of the kind of life I couldn't have. Being some wog fag way out west. Semi drug-addled. Limited money. Housing insecurity. Never having a wedding that my parents would dance at. Never having my own child that looked like the sum total of me and the boyf.

But one day I just became Costa, the man she used to work with. She said she regretted the affair. People were calling her a whore. She screamed. Tears.

Once I fucked my back trying to move her out of her own piss. She kept her hand on her Bible and I wished her a quiet death.

Because death can be quiet. Death can be as calm as the perfect triangle. Someone can look like they are taking a nap and then just like that *clicks fingers* they're gone. But not Fufu.

At times Alzheimer's is a hell you don't know you are in. Meanwhile, people look down onto you, into you. Going, going, gone. They aren't the people that you recognise. Horror replaces the sweetness and there isn't recognition in their eyes, just this scared look. So the Syrinapx kept looking better and better. Opiates numbed the kinds of pain that a chiropractor couldn't fix.

81RRON5

I used to work with this barman at the bowlo. Con. Sixty-three years old. Always doing something. Couldn't take a full breath standing still. He was six foot tall. Compact curls and great skin.

'The skips seem alright here,' I said to him once.

He stopped pouring Pepsi from the gun. Took some steps towards me and pointed a finger. 'Yeah. They're alright. But if they could get you fired, they would. Just for something to do.' He towered over me.

'Do you know Crown Street?' he said once. 'Six of us lived there when we came to Australia. In one of those terrace houses. We wanted to do renovations on the outside. But the Anglos reckoned we couldn't touch them. Those terrace houses have no light inside. No light. It was dank, Re. DANK!'

'Why couldn't you renovate?' I said to him. 'Cos they were heritage listed?'

'Fucking heritage listing. Arrr. In Greece you can't dig a hole to bury a communist without uncovering ancient shit!'

'Hey, watch it, mate.' I raised my hand. 'Some of those buildings are over seventy years old.'

I used to work on the pokies. Deros and reffos would put a dollar in the Emerald Oriental Bride machine. Ask for free Pepsi and coffees. I'd never talk, only fake smile and ask them, 'What can I get for you?'

We had homos come in sometimes. Around Christmas and New Year's, the poofs who came good came home. They wore thin blue polos tucked into tight beige chino shorts with braided patent belts so shiny you'd think the leather was sweating. Their families dared them to drink VB. They came to the bar heroically.

'One domestic drink, please,' the queer would say to me.

'One what?'

'You know – a cup of beer drink,' he'd say.

'Did you lose a bet?'

'For realzingtons. How did you know? Is the drink called the Victorian Bitters?'

'I'll call you Odysseus 'cos this is your *Iliad*.'

'I don't know what that means. But I'm DJing later at this party.'

'Really?'

'Yeah. A collective of lesbians renovated an underground sewer that was a biohazard site. It's really cool.'

'That. Sounds. Sydney.' I reached over the bar and tapped him on the chest. I took his money. Gave him back his change and held my hand in his hand. Eye contact too long.

Turned around and Con was there, folded arms.

'What are you doing, Re?' said Con. He looked at me like he was trying to figure me out.

'What do you mean?' I said.

He clicked his mouth and shook his head.

I went back to cleaning the fridge doors. Putting soapy water on the glass, using a squeegee to get it off.

Sometimes I'd set up the bar at 9 am. Morning shift duties included putting out the bar runners, long plastic-based protectors that are really advertisements. They catch the head of beer that drips down the side of the frosted glass.

After filling up the ice buckets we opened for trading. Our first customers were shift workers finishing off for the night. Truckers who'd down a few schooners and shoot the shit with me. 'Whaddaya know?' they'd ask.

'I know what I see,' I'd say to them. They kept the banter light, didn't ask me about girlfriends. Most of them had been inside; now they were flying the straight and narrow. Still had quick darting eyes. Still had their back to the wall out of habit.

Some customers came in early, got a couple of schooners. Watched reruns of the cricket. Dreamed of the good innings they ran in life.

Nice Arms Pete came in on the reg. I was keen as. Sometimes when I served him he'd hold my gaze too long. Too musculoskeletal, I'd think.

Once he leaned back on a pokie chair and put his legs in between the machines. Pushed a button for service, wanted a coffee. Was confused by our lack of skim milk.

I put on my straight-acting wog boy accent and said, 'Full fatty cow milk is good for bulking phase.'

Later he came to the bar.

I kept looking at his arms. They were alabaster with blue veins that ran down them like rivers.

'You mirin'?'

He folded them over the bar; the biceps popped. He winked at me like we had a conspiracy going.

'Just call me Nice Arms Pete,' he said.

My face hella hot, I wanted to giggle.

I signed up Nice Arms Pete to club membership. He held the pen too far up from the nib and pressed too hard on the form. More than once I had to ask him what this or that word meant. He stood in front of the computer as I typed in his deets. The form in front of me had his childish scrawl.

'And what are these numbers here?' I asked him.

'That ain't numbers, that's my suburb – Birrong.' He stepped from side to side, leaned over the computer I was working on. The B looked like an 8 and the G looked like a 5. 81RR0N5.

We took his photo five times. Some of the pics had white crud around the side of his mouth. Told him to hold the digital camera up high, angle his head down and look up into the camera. That worked. Nice Arms Pete got a membership and pretty photo thanks to selfie angles.

Barman Con figured it out. He saw the way I purposely wouldn't talk too much when I served Nice Arms Pete. Caught us talking just a bit too much near the pokies when I thought no one was around.

'Don't mess with the natives,' Con said to me. That was the day he had a heart attack. He was carrying two schooners of dark beer to the pokies. I thought he'd slipped and fallen over. The Tooheys Old made puddles in the worn-out carpet. The beer spread out slowly, got soaked up by his hair. That's when I called triple zero.

I left a bit after that. Me and Nice Arms Pete moved in together. Occasionally we still went back to play the pokies.

RODD STREET

Me and Nice Arms Pete sat in front of Hercules' Odyssey, waiting for gold wreaths. The swelling on my face had receded, I looked like a bar-room brawler. Held a buzzer that would go off when our chilli prawn pizza was ready. It was almost seven, the sun was done, our world was lit up by pokie hyperlight.

Sounds all around cushioned us with whirrs and clicks.

Sounds all around us were eight-bit choruses and synth faux movie tracks, all the drama and excitement of losing your rent money.

We kept waiting for the gold wreaths to line up. The graphic reels spun and gave us two in a row of Hercules flexing his bicep. When it appeared twice Nice Arms Pete flexed his arm like the image on screen. What can I say? Biceps on the screen and biceps in real life made me animated.

'Your guns coming along, eh? Nice, brah,' I said.

His muscle tone increased. One or two kilos of lean muscle. He'd always been lean but naturally thick. Grew up like a night creature so he didn't get much sun. Kept his skin nice.

'My dad had a weight set at home,' he said. 'He got me working out when I was a kid. I stopped for a while.'

'Thought your dad wasn't around?' I asked.

'I dunno, can't keep track of everyone.' Nice Arms Pete shrugged.

We got a little feature on the machine. Three golden fleeces lined up. I wondered what the hell golden fleeces had to do with Hercules. It started a whirl.

I punched the air. Nice Arms Pete was happy too so he put his hand around the back of my neck and closed his grip hard. Tensed my back and resisted it, but then accepted it. Shut my eyes, mouth opened a little and my face tilted towards the ceiling. I took long breaths into the pit of my gut and submitted my body to his version of a hug.

A few machines down from us was an old geri lady playing Mermaid's Revenge. She looked over at us and

I heard her say in our direction, 'How lovely! A nice massage after a hard day's work!' She raised a black cup of tea to her mouth and sipped at it.

'Would you like a massage too?' said Nice Arms Pete, and the old lady laughed.

The buzzer in my hand vibrated. I went to get the pizza. Walked through the club. Old school Aussie customers downing schooners in a shout. When the local area went wog, all the skips that could afford it became part of the 'white flight'. They couldn't stand to see their fibro bungalows being turned into double-storey brick veneer with white Corinthian columns, so they sold up and left the Lebs, wogs and reffos. Moved out to cheap beachside suburbs dotted along the coast. The ones that couldn't afford to leave became our customers. They acted like jackals in the TAB. About mid-fifties. Ex local football stars who had resigned themselves to the three Ds: diabetes, divorce and drunkenness.

That night there were heaps of wogs with families around, chicken coops they built around themselves. Collared shirts tucked into jeans. Women in tight pants and fitted shirts. Multicoloured heels that made them tower over the men.

When I was walking past the bar I noticed that a wog guy was fighting with a Leb chick. There were three jugs of soft drink in front of them. The Leb chick tried giving the barman the money and the wog guy kept pushing her hand away.

At the bistro I handed my flashing buzzer to a preppy kidling. Fresh skin. Maybe sixteen. Name tag read 'Piotr'. 'Here's your Tony Soprano . . .' The box had a picture of a fat swarthy cartoon man twirling a moustache.

'I didn't order that,' I said.

'That's what we call a seafood chilli pizza here,' said the kid. He smiled.

'Some vowels missing from your name.' I pointed to the name tag.

The kid laughed. 'Are you in the pokies?'

'Yeah, I am.'

'With that tall guy? The one with the nice arms?' asked the kid.

'Alright, calm down, bro.' I pushed my hand down, palm flat, gesture mimicked what I said.

The kid smiled deviously. He turned around. Scuttled back into the kitchen.

I walked through the club again. Looked around to see what was going on. No one on the dining side of the club was in trackies. There were families sitting at long tables with linen. Grandparents. Young mums. Old mums. Balding fathers with athletic bodies. Pretty teenage girls and boys staring at their smartphones. Children running around. I focused on a young Greek family that had a modestly dressed girl sitting in the corner. The dad of the family noticed me checking them out. He growled at me but I wanted to say, 'Don't worry, bro. I wasn't checking your daughter out – I was checking you out.'

Back in the pokieverse the golden fleeces were still paying off.

'One Tony Soprano . . .' I said to Nice Arms Pete. I sat on the stool next to him and opened the box. 'Things from the earth and things from the sea – all on a pizza – together at last.'

I offered a slice to the geri lady in front of Mermaid's Revenge. She smiled; her lipstick was messy, some of it was on her teeth. Her eyes crinkled. A nanosecond nod.

'Oh, thanks so much, darl . . . but I'm not very big on the ethnic food.'

'You mean pizza?'

She cocked her head like a reptile. Looked at me through the side of her eye.

We wolfed it down. Nice Arms Pete gulped Pepsi Max in between slices. The ethnic jibe reminded me about Bruno. I talked about him to Nice Arms Pete, told him how much I liked the old cunt, told Nice Arms Pete some stories about him.

When Bruno was a child he had to take the ferry every day from his island to get to school. His teacher held a wooden ruler and would rap boys on the hand if they spoke out of turn. He learned about the scientist Marconi, who in 1930 flipped a switch in Genoa that turned on the lights in the Sydney Town Hall via wireless radio.

'In his head that linked his world and Australia,' I told Nice Arms Pete. 'And Australia to him.'

When he got to Australia, Bruno worked in the tin bellies of freezing warehouses, punching into time clocks. Buying weekly tickets for the same train for years. And the break was the man he met called Pete. The blond local sat next to Bruno one lunch break. Befriended him. Introduced him to hotels serving beer after work. Men like them would sit around and spend money on shouting each other drinks. Bruno learned and avoided this ritual. Saving money. Buying his first property outright, while the rest of them kept buying their mates rounds.

'So how many properties does he have?' asked Nice Arms Pete. He was smashing the pizza.

'Seems like he sold a few, kept a few. Money must be somewhere.'

'The deal with him and that guy?' Nice Arms Pete was talking about the blond man.

After five years in the same factory Bruno and Pete had to leave. Other workers started to talk about the Italian who smelled of salt water and the unmarried Aussie, the way they would sit together during lunch breaks, make beelines for each other at morning tea and walk home together at the end of the day. A co-worker found them talking on the roof of a car park. They were standing next to each other, looking out. They weren't touching but they enjoyed the line of sight in front of them, that made people start talking. So they both left the factory. Bruno had a small amount of money saved. They took a road trip down south to see if they could get a job on the state-funded hydroelectric projects. They slept under moistened bush. Koalas fighting above them. Freshwater river baths were the best for cleaning. Salt water left a hardness to fabric and skin itched when it got sweaty.

We finished the pizza. The machine was on a feature. Nice Arms Pete and I took a cigarette on the balcony.

'So was Bruno and that guy a thing?'

'The answer is yes, but he talks around it. I have to interpret him based on what isn't said.' I walked to the railings.

'And the money and the rest of the property . . . got deets?' Nice Arms Pete looked away but waited for the answer.

'No kids . . . so don't know where his treasure went,' I said, exhaled smoke like a barrier between us.

A sigh came out of Nice Arms Pete.

'So many things you want to know, eh?' My hand traced the metal railing we were leaning on.

'Can't be fucked answering that one,' said Nice Arms Pete.

'Lots of questions you don't answer,' I touched my shiner. Put my other hand on the bicep of my partner, almost commenting on his roid change. I looked across the bowls green. Beyond where the houses ended, chrome clouds stalked the horizon.

Back in front of Hercules' Odyssey we continued playing, no conversation. Last thing I said still hung around. I wanted answers about the guy in the Hell Red Commodore who'd dropped him home the other night.

That night, I got my fill of happiness. The pizza, the pokies. Guess I wanted the rollercoaster down.

The pizza teen Piotr from the bistro came up behind us. He pointed to the empty pizza box sitting between machines. 'Want me to get rid of that box?'

Nice Arms Pete did a slow nod at the kid, talked more with his eyes.

'It was good, yeah?' said the kid. His lips reached from ear to ear.

'Hey, I used to work here with Con,' I said.

Both Nice Arms Pete and the kid turned to look at me. The puppy raised his eyebrows; the crinkles on his forehead gave me a glimpse of what he was like at school when the teacher asked him a hard question.

'Con, the barman. I used to work here. So . . .'

'Sorry. I'm too young to know any of the old people,' said the kid in a voice that was just a little too high to be nice.

'Thanks so much,' said Nice Arms Pete to the kid, who blushed.

'Hopefully see you again.' The kid spoke like Schweppervescence. He winked. Walked off. Nice Arms Pete faced the pokies again, content. My mouth fell.

'What?' said Nice Arms Pete. Abrupt. Roid rage boiled.

The old geri lady became rattled by us, how our tone increased and drowned out the synthetic pokie songs.

I addressed questions to Nice Arms Pete through a clenched smile. My fury escalated. Post questions came the accusations. What I said didn't matter. Words deleted. Syntax of no importance. It was the effect, it was the feeling. And I wanted to make his cheeks fluster, to frustrate him out of words. He responded by grabbing my throat, lifting his paw to strike me.

Looking back it was good that security showed up to kick us out. It united us as we left through the entrance. We hissed at management on the way out. Nice Arms Pete kicked over a pot plant.

'That plant's not even real,' said Nice Arms Pete.

Security guards stood there, their hands crossed in front of their crotches.

Later that night, I looked over the mountain of Nice Arms Pete snoring. In my palm two little blue moons. I swallowed them. The memory of two white columns grabbing at my throat, causing pain and releasing it.

BRUNKER ROAD

Nice Arms Pete in beast mode was a devil's meal. I liked to run my finger over the two segments where his butt cheeks met his waist. Thought that was what kept me there.

He was always stretching. Waiting for water to boil and pushing his arms out in front of him. Watching a sitcom and stretching his lats. In line for the ATM and extending his legs like a triangle.

I would get dressed, head to work. Nice Arms Pete said he was going to the gym.

Always thought that he would be going to the Belmore PCYC. Might have got his cardio on, ridden his bike and then chained it to a fence post, paid a small fee to the front desk staff. Probably there was some interaction. He might have smiled and asked if there was anyone in there and then paid with coins he kept in his zippered pocket.

Thought that he might have been in a room by himself. Nice Arms Pete facing a wall, stretching into his back, hands pushing against exposed brick or even concrete walls with that weird stalactite stuff. His eyes picking out specks on the floor while feeling the burn through his lats.

He might have been breathing into that stretch when another scent hit him. A body odour that he breathed fully through his mouth and nose. Scent tickling his lips. Even the back part of his tongue might have freaked out and pushed onto the roof of his mouth. The scent would have been powerful, as strong as a pumping bicep almost ready to explode – pow! Shoot with awesome power! The scent might have gone deep, too deep into the lower parts of his chest, causing some awkward coughing, and then stirring his crotch because his peen was probably connected to the animal part of him – the way men's stomachs are connected to their heart. Would have felt that smell on his diaphragm. And he would have tried to think what it reminded him of. And because Nice Arms Pete isn't that creative he would have thought of pepper clouds or maybe the labourers on the farm where he grew up. The way those men dripped sweat of food and hard work. That smell would be some weird association for his on-the-border-of-homoville teen memories when his dick first started getting aroused by the blue singlets those labourers wore. Maybe.

Might have shook his head once or two or three times. The way a dog does when it eats something too hot.

If Nice Arms Pete turned around he might have seen him, standing there in front of a mirror. The upside-down pyramid man. With his soft olive skin, probably smooth as butter all over in that gym rat way – which is the opposite of me, with my washed-out jaundice yellow and my giant pores. This gym rat would have had small pores. And Nice Arms Pete probably looked at him and thought, 'His pores are so much smaller than my current boyfriend's and he is doing isolation exercises! Ding!' The upside-down pyramid man probably had a jawline that might have been cut by a laser. His irises might be permanently massive, taking in all the light and all the attention away from his body, so that when they made accidental eye contact, Nice Arms Pete might have thought, 'It's like looking at a cartoon character's eyes, perhaps from a Japanese animation, and his eyes are so unlike my current boyfriend's.'

I knew Nice Arms Pete had a kind he liked, a regular go-to on his dating résumé. Italian guy from Blacktown. Turkish guy from Auburn. Nice Arms Pete thought all his men were different but they were the same. Twig-skinny Viet. Pacifica dude from Cabra that was totes shredded. Did the same things on a bunch of them. Hands on their throats. White fingers vice grip turning necks pink. He wrung the necks of all his fucktoys.

But Nice Arms Pete wouldn't want to do those choking violent things with this unit. Nice Arms Pete probably wanted to climb him. Ride that horse saddleless. Make me jealous on purpose.

Perhaps they talked to each other at the gym. Perhaps not. Perhaps Nice Arms Pete could hear the Clang! Grunt! Clang! Grunt! of the Olive-Skinned Hulk as he did his sets, because of course this guy was probably a Clang! Grunt! kind of guy. Maybe he corrected Nice Arms Pete's form and later they'd start talking in the showers and Nice Arms Pete might say, 'Oh, thanks for that help before,' and the Olive-Skinned Hulk might have said, 'Grunt!' and they would have laughed and flirted and laughed and flirted.

Or maybe the Olive-Skinned Hulk was just silent as a cascade of water fell over his body and made it glisten like some kind of tanned killer whale and others in the shower were mirin' his ripped back, comparing it to the crinkles on a scrunched-up piece of paper. And then maybe when Nice Arms Pete went and had a shower, he watched the Olive-Skinned Hulk getting dressed through the curtains of water, sneaking looks at him like a creep, like the way he used to sneak looks at my butt when I was in the shower. Which was totally okay when he did it to me because we were a thing, but I'm not sure how I feel about him doing it to others.

I thought about the way Nice Arms Pete got dressed in the mornings or after showers. Maybe when he finished in the shower he did his weird old ritual of putting his socks on first and then pulling up the Y-fronts. As he stood around the locker room in socks and underwear he might have looked down and seen the licence that the Olive-Skinned Hulk dropped when he was trying to flee all the pervy eyes. Perhaps Nice Arms Pete picked up the licence, thought of himself being sweet and doing a Good Samaritan deed, decided to deliver the licence to its owner personally because damn it! What if that poor and extremely attractive man needed to drive somewhere and got pulled over by a tough but semi-racist police officer and got a fine or was taken into the cop shop? Nice Arms Pete would have been so sad . . . that he wouldn't be able to see him again for a while.

Probably Nice Arms Pete jumped on his bike, rode through the streets and turned down a street that had three-metre-high red bottlebrushes. Then maybe he would have looked at the commission houses across the road and wondered if he could find the residence, if he could find the place that this Olive-Skinned Hulk lived in. Was it some kind of Fortress of Solitude? Were the bricks made out of protein that his hero could nibble and munch on?

Nice Arms Pete would roll up to a line of three houses, all of them identical, and he wouldn't understand that they were all designed and built after World War II in the California bungalow style, so his brow would probably furrow in confusion and it probably looked really cute. His legs may or may not have been aching because he may have done some squats before and that area may or may not have been hilly and he would have felt the burn in his legs, simultaneously angry and relieved that his workouts were going well.

Maybe he went straight up to the house and knocked on the door, or maybe he sat on his bike across the street or hid behind a tree and watched the houses.

If he did sit across the street, he probably could identify the differences in some of the houses and write them off as cosmetic rather than important. Perhaps he wouldn't understand what kind of person lived in one of the bungalows that was painted grey all over, that horrible basic taupe, fawn, mushroom or ecru. He wouldn't understand that this taupe colour meant that people were starting to gentrify the neighbourhood and that there was a Facebook group called Taupe Abodes of the Inner West where disaffected people could complain about this paint colour as a symptom of the problem with society.

If he did sit across the street, he probably watched as a hybrid car or luxe jeep parked in front of the ecru abode and a MILF in activewear got out of it. She probably pulled out a stroller that cost more than three weeks' worth of most people's wages. The stroller itself would have been matt silver with big offroad wheels. It might have been a baby stroller or it might have been the capsule that Jor-El himself used to send his son from Krypton to Earth. She might have then taken her child and pushed it or carried it into the house and Nice Arms Pete might have kept looking at the house next to it.

Perhaps the house Nice Arms Pete was looking at wasn't a California bungalow. Perhaps it was a recently constructed duplex that was the same colour on one side as it was on the other. Perhaps the Olive-Skinned Hulk lived in a duplex or maybe where the California bungalow that used to be there was knocked down and his wog parents – his father some kind of merchant or builder – had replaced it with a three-storey, double-brick job with Corinthian columns, and the Olive-Skinned Hulk worked three days a week for his dad's business and was confused about his sexuality in the way that young wogs who are stuck in the family business can be.

Or maybe the Olive-Skinned Hulk lived in a house that once belonged to his parents. And if Nice Arms Pete knew what to look for he could see the lemon trees and olive trees in the front yard. Maybe then, just as Nice Arms Pete was looking at this house that may have been a duplex, a bungalow or an ethnic McMansion, the postman would come, the postman might get off his bike, the postman might ring the doorbell twice.

There might have been a snarl. Bark, two dogs exploding from the back fence or maybe the yap yap yap of a toy puppy. Perhaps the high wooden gate at the side of the house heaved as the dogs tried to push it down and then, after ringing twice, the postman might have jumped on his bike and cycled away down the pavement lined with bottlebrushes.

For all I know Nice Arms Pete became curious and decided to creep into the front yard of the house. For all I know Nice Arms Pete leaned his bike against a fence and went over to the house and looked in the windows, or maybe he sat in the front yard smoking a cigarette. Perhaps he looked at the lemon trees and wondered why there were all these old plastic bottles with precision-cut circles on the side. And in the plastic bottles there would have been a brown liquid that filled them a quarter way up and there were these clouds of dead insects in them. And he would've wondered why these plastic bottles hung on the lemon tree like some futuristic insect mass grave. Because that's the kind of thing he wondered.

Maybe he got up and left and went back another day.

Maybe he got up and the Olive-Skinned Hulk was just walking into his house carrying a bag of lean meat and broccoli. Maybe Nice Arms Pete said, 'Hi, I am from the gym!' and then waved the Olive-Skinned Hulk's licence and they went inside and Nice Arms Pete gave him back his licence and they fucked and then jumped in the Hell Red Commodore. I dunno.

BURWOOD ROAD

I woke before dawn, couldn't get back to sleep. Rubbed my face on a dirty pillow. Went outside for a smoke. The white wings of a night-bird cut across the sky, it hollered overhead, disappeared over a red roof. I read it as a sign, needed a must-see. The must-see was Mama.

Called a few times before she picked up the phone. If she was as psychic as she claimed she would have answered, instead my baba yelled, 'Speak!' into the receiver. I hung up then called again. When she finally answered, she gave instructions and a whinge.

'This isn't a life! It's a hell! Come at midday! When he has gone. But don't stay too long. Stay for a while at least! Don't be here when he comes back! Alright?'

she said. Heard her slam the phone down, two pieces of plastic crashing. Dial tone in my ear.

My baba, that's who she complained about. He was an excuse not to give up smoking, someone to give the silent treatment, someone to blame when the taps leaked. Every day she said her prayers and watched Nikos Xanthopoulos on YouTube. In between she cooked and her husband lectured.

When I lived with them, the first thing I would see in the morning was a poster of a young Elvis just above my bed. I got lost in his sullen look to camera, the soft black-and-white focus of the era. After my Elvis phantasm I'd go straight to the backyard. Walk past Mama in the kitchen, sitting on an orange vinyl chair. On the clear-plastic-coated table, she would gently prepare her dough baby. Beyond our fence I could hear freight trains go by while inside my dad lectured Mama.

'The prime minister is cutting my pension! Do you know how expensive a coffee is at Gloria Jean's?' he asked her.

Then I'd hear a thud, thud, thud and thud – the sound of her punching the dough. Her grey helmet of hair was parted in the middle.

'It is a well-known fact that a woman has the brain the size of mango, the man has the size of the watermelon,' he would say, and I would hear more thud, thud and thud.

'There is one problem with that,' she said, picking strands of grey hair from the dough. 'A mango fits in a woman's head – a watermelon doesn't fit in a man's head.' Outside the train would finish passing by and birds returned to sit on the wire.

When I lived with them, I spent most of my time away from them. One night I went to the shittiest gay bar in the inner west. It was the home of Priscilla, it was the home of Roey and Goey. Instead of shacking up with some leather-pants-wearing out-of-towner, I reclaimed my dignity. Went home. Woke Mama as I entered the house. We both went outside to the back table. She made us cups of tea. Bludged Winnie Golds off her. Talked about weather and nonsense and cousins in Greece. Kept extinguishing our cigarette butts in the bonsai plants she was trying to grow. She asked if I had a girlfriend. Then she told me I was gay. She said to me, 'Don't tell your father.'

Three months later I sat him down at the kitchen table. Told him I was a πουστι. His response was concise. 'We had a poofter in the army. He kept losing his wallet.' Then he blanked me for two years. In the kitchen I would pour milk on my Weet-Bix and he would wait for the kettle to boil. Both of us had our backs to each other. I would finish in the toilet and wait for him to leave the bathroom so I could wash my hands. We passed each other at the door, tilting to the side, his eyes up, my eyes down. In the mornings before my dad went to get coffee at Roselands he would fight with my mother. I would wake in my single bed, pull down my green and gold quilt that celebrated the '83 America's Cup victory, stand at my bedroom door while my mother yelled at my father in the backyard, 'Why don't you lick my sweet cunt?'

To escape all this, I went on long walks around Belmore. I walked all the way down to Cooks River, passing houses that I wished I owned. Houses that had neat front yards, scrappy dogs barking behind fences, polite hedges, trimmed blue grass, fruit trees in the yard. They had shiny Japanese cars parked in the driveway.

After the houses tour, I would walk up past my old primary school and along Burwood Road to the train station. My headphones would block out the traffic sounds. I stood on the bridge of Burwood Road, leaning on the fence, looking down at the trains coming from the city at peak hour. All along the fence, fathers leaned and waited for their daughters. Mothers with prams waited for men in black and grey pants, collared shirts and ties. As they walked up the stairs, sometimes their socks had a bright colour on them, maybe love hearts or polka dots. Toddlers would run up to their fathers. Those afternoon-almost-nights, everything not in my world was right.

I'd had enough of Baba for eternity.

Left there and moved into a temporary share house situation with a twink.

Found him on a sex app. We met for coffee in public, played it straight while I ordered a latte for myself and macchiato for him. In a hidden park in Bankstown we sat on swings. He confessed to me, Catholic guilt strong in him.

'Where did you go to school?' I asked.

'I was homeschooled,' he said with a lisp, looked up at me with green-grey eyes.

'Shut up . . . But you are so handsome.'

'Thanks,' he said.

'So you think you are handsome?'

'Oh, um . . .'

'Where were you raised?'

'Here, in Bankstown.'

'If you're from Bankstown, why are you white?'

He didn't get it.

Told Twinkness that I'd found a place later that week. At midnight on a Friday he fled his room through an open window and moved into the second room of the house. We'd sit on Bunnings outdoor furniture and he'd tell me about what was going on in his life. Main issue: parents stalking him. A bearded Irish Catholic in a ute driving up and down Oxford Street on Friday nights. A redheaded matron in a grey dress hiding behind the aisles in Woolworths. I used to bite my top lip and console the little orphan, ask him if he got The HIV yet and who's on The Meth yet and what's the new drug?

'Maybe, everyone and LSD has made a comeback.'

'LSD? What is this? Year ten?' I'd say. 'Spoken to the parental units?'

'I saw my dad . . .' He'd cup his milk neck with a palm.

'Good. How was that?' I'd puff on a jay.

'No. Like I just saw him as I was walking to the train station. He was in the ute following me.' A strawberry hair waterfall flopped over his eyes.

Told him everything would be okay. Thinking while looking at him, 'Idiot, don't listen to me, I don't know shit.'

'Did you watch *Mommie Dearest* yet?' I asked. Took it upon myself to educate him. All things mo.

'I thought the way the mother treated her children was really sad,' said Twinky.

I left him to move in with Nice Arms Pete. Wondered what happened to him, but with his floppy hair and milk skin, I reckon he shacked up with some older corporate in Darlo – a twinky-type trophy boyf.

•

Driving to my parents' house killed my life. The Hume Highway was my arterial between Western Sydney and the up-and-coming Belmore – but to me it was already old and gone. Was in two minds about it. Devils versus angels. Told myself something comical about seeing Mama. *I'll laugh at and with her!* But the other side of me was over cute, so I puffed another Fine Cut White. Then I was on Burwood Road. Cafes hosting players from the Sydney Bulldogs. Pure muscle hulks posing for camera phones with plus-size pre-teen woglets. Passed the leagues club with its fake rock three-tiered waterfall that spewed flames hourly at night, attracting high-roller Asian gamblers. A new smoothie bar had just opened. Glammas in Lorna Jane, full face of make-up, living the dream and working off excess pregnancy weight between cigarettes.

I passed the open sewer that cut across the whole burb and spewed rainwater into Cooks River. As a kid used it as a shortcut to different parks or a place to try my first cigarette (aged thirteen) then pull my first bong (aged sixteen). In my twenties used to pull guys down in there to fuck.

Drove past a row of houses me and a friend used to pass on the way home from school. At each letterbox my friend would pull out the envelopes, rip them in two and throw them into the air. My friend would laugh through his nose. His name was Telly. Back then he was a scrawny guy, little legs. Once he lay stiff as a plank and I benched him whole.

Did a little tour of the old neighbourhood. Buckley's of seeing anyone that I knew. Drove into streets and back lanes, remembered a house, the previous owners were Greeks. Had some vague kin connection to the greaseballs. The Haus of Wog still had olive trees in the yard, a bungalow all modified into concrete column splendour. A garden: half decoration, half food. It was an investment property for the owners. For a while a junkie couple lived there and let it go to shit. Marijuana plants had replaced their tomatoes, the junkies punched holes in walls. When I was in year two, a blond kid called James lived there with his family. We were in the same class and if I knew what love was back then, I would have said I fell in love.

Past the old house and up the road were the gates of the old primary school, Belmore North. The gates had large brick overhangs, old gothic buttresses. Next to them, a straight pale eucalyptus tree grew up. Broke through black asphalt that failed to keep it in the ground.

When I was a pup I'd arrive early and take the leaves off the eucalyptus tree. I'd rip along the lines of the leaf veins. The smell of the oil reminded me of eucalyptus lollies in my father's car. They sat in a small rectangular tin. I used to shake them and hear hard translucent yellow raining against metal as we drove around a maze of cul-de-sacs.

Just past the gates was the paperbark that had been there forever. I stopped the car, got out. The tree was carved with names. Two names stuck out: *James* and *Telly*. The letters overlapped, sewing them together. My name was still there too. *Bux*. All in angles, the X larger than any of the letters preceding it.

•

Back in the day three synthetic horns meant the beginning of school.

We would line up next to the classroom and wait for our teacher. My place was at the end of the line, with James and Telly.

I remember James's blond hair looked alive. Me and Telly had dark skin and dark features. We had not-from-here rituals. James had an earring, a golden sleeper. Expensive sneakers he called kicks. He wore them with athletic socks pulled high. And he bought his lunch every day: canteen lamingtons, sausage rolls that flaked with pastry and meat pies; strawberry milk, pink and delicious, and bottomless cola. We all looked at him, jealous.

Telly was from a family of Cyprian reffos. His skin looked like it was made of copper. So did his hair. He was the first to grab James. Telly was the fastest at Bull Rush. Skipping and weaving in between the others. He could balance soccer balls on his feet, spin basketballs on the tips of his fingers and use his Bull Rush skills as a league wing. He was good at sport, so I thought I had no chance of friendship with James.

Telly forced the friendship. But for me and James it grew. It started one time when our teacher, Ms Kibble – or was it Mrs Killball? – paired us together. Ms Kibble or Mrs Killball was modern, with dark slicked-back gelled hair, dark kohl around her eyes and drop earrings. She was ahead of herself. Made sure that we spent more time doing activities that grew our self-esteem.

One time we had to draw each other. I studied James closely, an excuse to stare at him. I drank him in, finding the right yellow for his hair and the perfect pink for his cheeks. As James sat for his portrait his eyes were away somewhere. By accident I drew one of James's legs disproportionately larger than the other.

'Bux! Look how big you made my leg!' James huffed. There was a smile on his face. 'I think it's funny you made me a spastic.'

It clicked for me, my emotions caught in a net.

When it rained – loud like a snare drum on the library roof, making it hard to read – we sat closer, our mouths in each other's ears, almost touching hands while we held a book.

Waiting in line for class to start was the time when most things happened. Once I heard Telly and James talking.

'Cherry bombers are so much better than metal conkers,' said James.

'What are you talking about? Metal conkers are the b—' said Telly, but James interrupted him.

'My dad who is a mechanic said that you pretty much get metal conkers anywhere. Anywhere where they work with engines and stuff.' James wiped his nose with the back of his hand. Left a snail trail on his skin.

Against the demountable wall: Telly, James and I would share the last three spots. James and Telly would usually be next to each other; I would stand behind them.

'Don't you think I'm your best friend?' said Telly to James.

'Sure you are,' James answered then he winked at me. 'Sure. You're my best friend, Telly.'

One day I was sitting on the carpet in the classroom. The windows of the demountable were open. A hot slow breeze stirred. Asked Ms or Mrs or Miss where James was. She told me that he'd left. Muscles around my mouth went numb. She sat down next to me and put a hand on my shoulder. She tried to tell me something that would make me feel better: his parents had upped and moved to Queensland to 'be around more people like them'. Shat my pants that day. Was sent home at lunchtime wearing a raincoat in summer.

•

Three synthetic horns sounded. The lunch bell. I looked around the playground then fucked off outta there. Ran back to my car. Trying not to think what the teachers would do if they found a weirdo like me on the edge of the playground.

CECILIA STREET

I hit the street my parents lived on. Neat front yards, bottlebrushes on nature strips. Down a long driveway was my parents' single-brick shack. Pulled up to our yard and my baba, my one-bit dad, had left a ladder out near the macadamia tree. Underneath was a mini chainsaw. Pretty soon Mama came to the front door wearing a robe and slippers.

'Never lets them grow, he ruins all the trees.' She gestured with the mug in her hand, Nescafé flew around her. The trees seemed strangled. Fig tree missing limbs. The citrus trees had only three or four clipped branches.

Boxes that fell off the back of a truck are like an old wog's memory of war. Baba was a kid when he hid in a giant tree and watched his family home burn down. Now he chops down the places where that little boy hid.

'Do you want me to cook you something?'

I told myself to hold on, to show up. Pretty soon I'd answered her questions with one-word answers. But Mama still wanted something from me.

Really I wasn't there. I'm just her son. In her head Mama was singing old songs and she was all burned up because her dad died that morning. We went inside. I watched her body, all tense at the limbs, FrankenMama. Her eyebrows furrowed, they met in the middle, they arched and squiggled. The bottom part of her face didn't move, her lips and mouth carved by Phidias himself.

'Who told you?' I asked her in the kitchen.

'Theia Toula called me from Greece today but I knew last night.' Big bum and crook knees, Mama moved around the kitchen like it was an obstacle course. Poor thing had to hold onto the green vinyl chairs at the table to get around them. She went behind the white laminate bench, opened the cupboard above the stove. Pulled out a box filled with incense relics. Lit the incense in the thurible.

She kept turning off the radio every time I turned it on.

'No music for forty days! We are Greek and we are mourning!' She looked at me, cross.

She started throwing all the meats out of the fridge. Poured fresh milk down the sink.

'We are fasting for forty days! We are Greek and we are mourning!' Her arms spun as she washed the milk down the drain.

Got a can of oil, oranges, sugar, flour and baking soda to make Death Biscuits. As she squeezed the juice out of the oranges she told me about how my papou – her baba – yelled her name out last night while she slept. She bit her lips while kneading. 'That's when I knew he died.' Tears dripped down her chin, falling into the dough. Kept rolling the Death Biscuit dough, tears mashing into the yellow lump.

My eyes cast away from her. Black flies like dots of liquid hovered around a clean white windowsill. I remembered teenage visits to the mountain village every winter. Me and Mama stayed in the two-bedroom hut she was born in. My job was to roll Papou's cigarettes, light them and put them in his mouth. He was bedridden and would call for me from the other room. One time he spoke Καθαρεύουσα to me and said, 'I am an old lion and this lion's time has passed.' It sounded grander at the time.

Just above her eyes I recognised this pent-up tension about to erupt under the eyebrows. Her mind was full of a dream about her father. She told me about it.

Her mouth was open, she was lying on the cover of her queen bed. Dozing next to half-empty beer bottles. Her father's voice called to her, the voice became the bed around her, cotton sheets became the landscape of his moaning, increasing in decibels.

'Maybe he was trying to tell you something,' I said.

'His voice, urgent. It was an urgent yelling.' Mama looked at the clock. Much more time until her husband came back. Dread already looking for her.

'Maybe he was telling you something?'

'Tell me what? That my life sucks? That my husband is the worst and I have a son that never comes to see me?'

Mama had a window of reprieve from her husband, 11 am till the afternoon. He would go to coffee shops, buy things from the hardware shop, visit mechanics and see old friends. This was her time, in the house alone. He would always come back. Cursing objects. Cursing people. Looking for the stirrer to make Turkish coffee: 'Why don't people leave fucking things in their place?' Ma outside, picking rocket from the garden. He would slam a drawer shut, open another drawer, rummage through utensils, find something that didn't belong in the drawer – like a pen – and throw it against the wall. Then he would continue looking for his object while his wife's spine contracted at the sound of biros hitting plasterboard.

Your position was just living, living was limited joy, was what I understood from her. That explained rolling handmade pastry sheets five millimetres thick. Focusing on detail would relieve those everything-is-the-worst lectures from the man she married. He even complained about too much sun or sudden rains. 'Even the weather in this country is a poofter bastard!' Mama would hover over food that she was working on. Cut the pastry into the perfect square, hairless arm with a knife swooped over dough – like she was a doctor and it was flesh.

On her kitchen table sat a bowl of overripe bananas; the fragrance punched my nose.

'You want to eat?'

'I'm not hungry. At all,' I said.

Mama placed a plate of pie on the kitchen table in front of me. 'Just eat. You should go before he comes back.'

'You don't know if he is coming back.' Took off the pastry lid and picked at the moist garden greens in the spinach pie.

'He's too old now to leave again.' Crook knees went wonk around the kitchen. Worked too hard even to take care of herself. Never knew how.

'I'm not lucky enough for him to leave me this time.' A sigh from the bottom of her stomach.

Mama shot out some questions about my life.

'I'm working. He is at the gym,' I said. 'No time for nothing. No time for sex. But sex isn't the only part of the relationship.'

'Sex is the only reason you should be in a relationship.' Her hand dismissed me. 'Maybe you should go to the gym too, you look sick.'

I ate the crust of the pie last. My home zone was a processed-carb-free zone. Thanks, Nice Arms Pete. He kept a fridge lined with meat and protein powder.

We had a YouTube party. Moved my chair next to hers, we sat next to each other at the kitchen table looking at the laptop. Showed Mama my favourite killer whale videos. Glistening white and black body emerging from the afro of cold blue waters. Their jaws snapped at tiny waterbirds, then pummelled them against rocks.

'If I was a penguin I wouldn't go back into the water.' She looked over the rocky ocean. The veins on my arms became itchy.

'Because there's a killer whale in the water? But there is a chance that you'll be fine! That nothing will happen!'

Our day progressed. Cooking together. Kneading dough for a bake. I put out laundry on the Hills Hoist. Vacuumed under coffee tables. Got cans of tomatoes down from high shelves. Before we realised what time it was we heard the car pull into the driveway.

I ran to the front window, nudged the curtains and peered through the tiny gap. Baba's khaki green Kingswood looked worse than I remembered. Different coloured patches where repairs had been done.

Baba exited the car and I let go of the curtain. Turned around to see Mama's face. Her eyebrows knitted together.

I mirrored her panic. 'What should we do?' I said, shaking my limp hands.

Mama looked around. Took four steps towards her bedroom then turned.

'This way.' She pointed with her whole arm.

Went past her into the room.

Mama stood at the door. 'Stay here! Don't let him see you! Leave when you can!' She closed the door.

I sat on the bed. Emerald green bedspread shone. The dark brown bedhead glossy. Three things hanging on the wall. Two icons of the Holy Virgin and, in the middle of the Παναγίας, in framed glass were stefana from my parents' wedding. Stefana are two head-sized rings, white, decorated with pearls and connected with a satin ribbon. They are trophies found in every good Greek house, more important than any actual trophies or even achievements.

I sat and faced the dresser, which had a mirror on it and a shiny black jewellery box decorated with faux oriental patterns.

Heard Mama open the front door, then heard Baba yell from the driveway.

'Έλα εδώ, εφερα πραγματα . . .'

'I'm coming, I'm coming.' Her voice receded as she went down the driveway.

My neck twitched. It became tighter and tighter. A pain shot down the left side of my body.

The jewellery box was almost a foot long. I opened it and a tiny faceless plastic ballerina popped up and spun in circles. Sweet tinkling of the sounds took me back to my childhood. Reminded me of the time when Baba tipped over the kitchen table.

I was in the living room, using the couch as a mountain and the action figurines had to climb it. Mama called us for food. Three bowls of lentils on the kitchen table. The folks were having a conversation that became louder and louder. I held a hooded plastic skeleton – it leaped from couch to armchair. Heard Baba yell, 'Ταμισετα, σαν το πεθερό σας,' then the crash of the table being turned over. Flicked my head around, saw the back of Baba's head as he left the kitchen. Went to the kitchen; the table was turned over on its side, some of the bowls had been smashed. Brown soup dripping down the wall. Mama had straight black hair that fell all the way to her waist. She put her pale hands on her expressionless face. She went out of the kitchen, her blue dress trailing behind her. I stayed in the kitchen and pushed on the table to turn it back over. That didn't work so I went to the other side and pulled it from the legs. After I put it the right way up, I picked up the broken bowls and wiped away the soup. Went looking for Mama and found her sitting on the emerald green bedspread. Her head was bowed to the dresser and two columns of shiny black hair obscured her face. She looked up at the mirror on her dresser and then at the jewellery box next to it.

•

From being the height of the door knob to being someone sitting on the bed.

Outside the bedroom I heard my parents grumbling as they passed the door. Plastic shopping bags rustled. Footsteps thudded. Inside the jewellery box were long strands of fake pearls that had become a ball. In another section, three little pill bottles that I recognised. Picked up a white plastic bottle. Opened it. Placed two little blue pills in my hand, swallowed them, tilting my head back, moving throat muscles to get them down. Took out a handful of blue pills and pocketed them. They made a lump like a cluster of insect eggs. I. Could. Leave.

I opened the door a crack. Heard the sound of *Dr. Phil* from the television. Put my head between the door and the doorframe. Could see Baba's head on the armrest of the couch in the living room. Slid through the door, took careful steps to the front door. Made sure that the floorboards underneath the carpet didn't creak. Reached the front door. Fingers, light touch, turned door knob. Outside, the afternoon sun rolled out a path into the front yard. Turned around to see if Baba knew I was there – Baba didn't know shit. *Dr. Phil* was too exciting. Exited and left the door open, fearing the closing sound would jolt Baba. Ducked beneath the windows at the front of the house. Wondered how my dad, my baba, my one-bit old man, could watch so much *Dr. Phil* and still be a cunt.

PARK ROAD

Made a call to Nice Arms Pete that day, knowing that he was lying in bed. I imagined the way he looked. The bottom half of his face lit. Morning sun breaking through venetians and a curve of light under his lip. Holding the mobile to his ear, lying on his side, thin lips, two tiny canines jutting out for attention, bedsheets half on the floor.

'I'm always begging you for sex, like I'm some kind of dog,' I said. I'd just got off the bus and was loitering outside work.

'If anything you're a horny chimpanzee,' said Nice Arms Pete.

'A bonobo . . .'

'You mean a banana?'

'No, a bonobo.' Pulled the phone away from my ear, looked at the earpiece to see if there was anything in the way.

'I don't know what that is,' said Nice Arms Pete.

Walked into the work car park. Clutched at my neck. He still strangled me, even when I wasn't there with him.

'Are you calling for any reason?' said Nice Arms Pete.

'Had an amazing time with you last night. Needed it after the time I had with my mama.' My hands were still around my neck. Sides of my neck pulsed. Had to turn my torso to look either side of me, couldn't even hold my phone with my shoulder.

Silence on the other side of the phone. I listened to the silence with comfort, something that confirmed how I felt. Looking back, Nice Arms Pete read the silence as nada. A big zilch-o. The big empty and a hindrance to when he could get off the phone.

'Okay then. See ya later,' said Nice Arms Pete and ended the call.

I continued talking. 'Bye, miss you already,' I said to dead air.

Had to put on uniform of scrubs before I started work. Straight into the change room. Almost slipped on shiny powder blue tiles. Put my bag next to the porcelain white toilet that had a plastic black toilet seat.

Took off jeans and T-shirt, threw them into the corner next to the open shower. Full-length mirror and I could see the side of my neck flanks were blue and black. Last night: Nice Arms Pete's hands in a chokehold.

Twirled and looked over my shoulder. The cup of my back just above my hips had two circles the shape of thumbs. Last night: two thumbs dug into me, held my waist as thrusts punished me. Knees had partially formed scabs from being directly exposed to the kitchen tiles.

I remembered the sex, not in a straight line. There were the hot parts. Series of images and feelings. His pink nipples like two eyes, a heaving white chest as a face. On my knees, looking up at a waist without a face. In between these images were periods of black. No memory of moving from the kitchen floor to the bedroom, from pillow biting to reverse cowboy.

Went to the jeans that I'd thrown on the floor. Squatted down, hunched over them. Hands went inside each pocket. Found a fistful of pills, taxed from Mama's jewellery box stash. Picked the shiniest pill; the others had dust and lint and bits. Popped it in my mouth, turned on the sink faucet to sip water.

Sat on the toilet waiting for the painkiller buzz. My mobile rang. Got up, zoomed to my bag, rummaged through it. Found it under some clothes. It was from a private number and I assumed it was Mama. When I answered it all I heard was yelling on the other side of the phone.

'Ma!'

The yelling continued.

'Hey. Calm down. Speak.'

All I could hear was jumbled hybrid English and Greek, fluctuated decibels.

'Θεοδοσία σκασμός.' I replicated Baba's authoritarian manner. It shut her up. She started speaking in a tone I could understand.

'Εσύ . . . you took the . . . είναι δικά μου . . . why did you take them? Τα χρειάζομαι . . .'

'Mama, I swear I didn't. I swear I didn't take them.'

We talked over each other; it went on like this for a while. Theodosia all anger. I moved my mouth, lies coming out. Packed my bag with the jeans and T-shirt that I'd changed out of, kept talking. Then hung up on her. She called back. I turned the phone off. Put it deep in my bag, under all the clothes.

In the staffroom Agatha approached. She had this grin on her face. I was always scared when she smiled.

'I need to talk to you today.' Agatha direct but a butter-cream voice. Thought I was in trouble. 'Can you follow me please?' She wasn't asking.

She walked over to the meds closet. Opened the door with her swipe. Stood in the closet looking over the ledger of meds received and meds distributed. I held the door open while she checked the morning pill schedule. Her body lean from hard work. A muscular arse from all the walking, eight to ten hours a day, five days a week. But there was a little roll of flab where she tucked in her shirt. The back of her neck was a different texture to the rest of her. Her face slightly yellow from all the cigarettes.

'Is something wrong?' My voice was breaking, nervous, always wanting to please her.

She stopped looking at her ledger. Turned around. My eyebrows scrunched together, two little caterpillars. Felt my eyes sparkle as I looked at her, looked at the pills on the shelf behind her. She assessed me. Always assessing me. Must have picked up on my two gems ricocheting between her and the pills. Did a reading of me as confused and curious. Reached out, touched me on the arm. She knew that out of all the employees she managed, I responded to a mum touch. Stroked my forearm.

'No, no, no,' she reassured me. 'Nothing is wrong. We just might need you to take more shifts for a while.' Her mouth turned up at the edge.

I let out a sigh. Eyebrows back to normal. Felt release around the side of my mouth.

'Also, one more thing,' she added.

Held my breath again. Here it comes.

'Remember you have the training today. What to do in case of a fire. You were sick the day it happened so we got the trainer here just for you today.'

Nodded at her. 'Got it, boss.' A few weeks ago I'd taken a sickie just to bum around the house. I scanned the tone to figure out if she had any suspicions about my sickie.

'I have to get the next meds schedule at lunch. Can you come talk to me about the extra shifts at one o'clock?' She turned back to the ledger and rows of pills.

I stood there holding the door, still looking at her and the meds closet treasure cave. Among the other pain-killers were rows of Syrinapx. Camera shutter blink when I saw them. That perfect geometry of little packets lined up, lined up, lined up. The packets: bone-white back-grounds, a pale blue rectangle cut through the box like the Hume Highway cut through Yagoona.

Agatha kept doing her work and turned her head to the side. 'Thank you. That is all,' she said.

Backed out of the room, let the door glide closed.

•

I was about halfway through my morning duties, realised I had agreed to something that I didn't wanna do. Then did everything with asphalt arms. Jobs quickly, mind jumped: revenge and resentment. Fuck 'em! Fuck 'em all! I'm too fucking good for this! Do you know who I am? The reckoning will come! Treated the least aware residents like I was a removalist clearing a deceased estate. Gripped their ankles as if they were bone on a hunk of butcher's meat. The injuries that Nice Arms Pete gave me the night before were making my tasks hard. Dropped the residents into their wheelchairs, some landed with a thud on their coccyx. Pushed them way too quickly down the hallway, like there was a race to the recreation room, because there was a race for me and at the finish line were cigarettes, coffees and Syrinapx.

Reached Bruno in this mindset. This mindset of quick! This mindset of get it done! This mindset of do the jobs quickly and badly! Nursing my grievances. Casual hand raise was how I greeted Bruno, didn't even look him in the eye. Pulled off the sheets quickly. Went to move his legs around, get him into the chair. Grabbed his ankle quickly but Bruno's hand struck me on the wrist. Looked up at him; stood ice still and upper lip trembled.

'Heya, mate, what's wrong with you today?' said Bruno.

'Oh no, nothing. Thinking 'bout something else.'

'Probably thinking about big pussies or something. I used to think about pussies and big cocks, bloody wet all over the place,' he said.

I let out a long mouth breath.

'Bruno . . . know that man in the photograph?' I asked as I moved him into the wheelchair. Bruno's head turned around, tried to look at the photograph next to his bed. His head couldn't turn that far. Used his hands to rub his arms, squeezing blood back into them. Mouth made a low click.

'Roll me, roll me over there, I need to see him,' said Bruno.

I wheeled him around to the other side of the bed, where the nightstand was. Bruno looked at the photo of him and the man called Pete. The sundrenched beach they were on had a yellow, almost white dunescape. A rolling wave fell into eternity, frozen at that moment.

'In the factory, I was its head and he had to work under me . . . all the talking. But I loved the Bible, I loved the Bible reading and the book had dog ears but I kept a gold pen that a tailor gave me and I would put it in only the nova part that I would read.'

Bruno spoke fragments; I would have to interpret what he said by reading his face. Two cloudy eyes startled, his wrinkled skin a leathery ball, all scrunched up. Bruno picked up the picture frame. Skin seemed thin around his grey hands. They were held together with blue veins that ran across them like streets, keeping his digits in place.

'How would you like that?' Bruno's voice was soft as he slowly ran his index finger over the image memory. He massaged the neck of the man in the photo. His finger curled and rubbed, leaving his print on the glass.

'His neck and then his back, my hands would press open his arse . . .' Bruno sighed.

It wasn't the words that made me freeze. It was the words combined with the accent coming out of those wrinkled purple lips. It was the words combined with that low bass, coming from loose vocal folds.

'Come on, buddy,' I said, took the picture out of Bruno's hands, put it back onto the nightstand. It stood next to some tissues and the emergency button.

Rolled Bruno down the hall to the recreation room. Put him in front of the TV next to some of the vegetables. On the screen was a triangular figure in activewear and salt-and-pepper hair. Next to him were two shirtless bodies with abdominal muscles and orange skin. They moved on a torture machine, all the while holding the fakest of smiles, fluoro white shark teeth visible. I watched the screen, coveting. All around me the residents still kept living. Some talked in hushed tones, voices like the smoke of an extinguished candle. Some joked. Next to me Bruno was watching the screen too. He licked his lips. Opened his mouth to say something. Pushed his neck and chest up ready to make sounds. But then didn't. He sighed and shut his mouth. His eyes scanned the floor, stopped at a corner. I placed my hand on the man's shoulder, gently squeezed it.

•

During my break I opened my locker to get my smokes. Found my phone, picked it up and decided not to turn it on. I knew missed calls from Mama were waiting for me. Found my cigarettes and some pills hidden under my clothing. Had my head in my locker when Agatha started talking to me.

'How was your morning?' she asked.

I turned around. 'I need to talk about Bruno. Something is happening.'

Agatha moved from the lockers to the meds closet door. She swiped the tag and opened the door. She motioned to me to hold the door open while we talked.

'Yeah, well, he is starting to talk about sex more and more.' I let it hang there for a while. Couldn't see Agatha's expression anymore; she was facing the meds. Her pen went down a list on the paper attached to the clipboard. She ticked things off, wrote numbers in boxes. I turned my attention to the door handle. Moved it up and down. Put my finger on the latch and pushed it in. Held the latch with my finger for a while.

'Is he showing early signs?' said Agatha. Her face was turned away from me and so I noticed her voice. There were no soft edges to it. Wasn't girly. It was deep. Rough as guts. A world away from the Insta-teen baby voices most girls use these days.

'You would call being in his late eighties early?' I said.

I fingered the latch again. Pushed it in, seeing if it would hold there and it didn't. Eyed the meds again. The Syrinapx was lined up six to a row. Behind each plastic bottle were many others that seemed to go back into the closet, back to infinity.

'I gotta take a smoko now,' I said. Agatha grunted a bye, still busy with her ledger. Before I closed the door, she called out to me to wait.

'After that go to the meeting room for your one-on-one training.'

After the smoko I found the trainer waiting for me. Named Bob. Boring name but a clean kind of body. Pants cotton, blue, slim fit. Light brown leather winklepickers. One hundred and eighty centimetres tall with ninety-five kilos of protein bars and low-glycaemic carbohydrates. I knew the type. Bought in bulk, saved his pennies, a studio apartment too neat, bank loans for flat screens and OS trips, replica modernist furniture 'cos the real shit is too much.

We sat opposite each other. Our training began with a series of flash cards.

'Is this a Rorschach test or fire training?' I asked. He didn't laugh. Trainer Bob said ecksting-wish-aaah, inflection rising at the end. I had that Western Sydney patois that divided us two like the M5.

Trainer Bob's head was large, a giant egg on shoulders that looked like he used to be an athlete. He told me information that could save lives and I wondered about unzipping his fly and taking him in my mouth.

He went through different kinds of fire extinguishers. This one is water, don't use it on electrical fires. This one is powder, use it on electrical fires.

I held eye contact. Made gestures to him that he was above. Passing a form, our index fingers touched. I held it there for a while. Trainer Bob pulled away. I partially opened my mouth. Took my pencil, placed it in my mouth, drawing teacher's eye to it. But I was a crappy Lolita. Too old.

'There are no sprinklers in this place. You need to pay attention if there is a fire.' Then a sound came from his smartphone. I knew what that sound was. Our eyes met, recognition passed between us. I smiled. Trainer Bob's eyes opened a fraction, his mouth tight.

'You just got a message on your gay sex app,' I said. I leaned back into my chair and folded my arms.

'I'm a part-time photographer looking for models. That's all that is.' He arranged the cards in front of him just a bit too quickly.

In the little meeting room, we were supposed to be talking about fire safety, but graphs and training unit components couldn't erase what was outside. The different ways we spoke came and sat next to us on the plastic chairs. Our body shapes we inherited and fought for laid out on the table. Our money, the places we came from, ideas we picked up were all around us. In that shitty room. On display via our bodies. The accents when we said stuff. And the fact that I smelled like a deodorant that comes in a man can and he smelled like something that started with the words Eau de.

Moved my chair to sit next to him. When he tried to stop me I said that it felt too much like he was a cop interrogating me. My chair was placed close enough so I could push my thigh into his. He ignored it. Rolled his sleeves up. His forearm was like a drumstick, covered in thick black hairs. Hands that were square. Kept on showing me cards but I looked at his body parts.

'You're from the east, yeah? Come out to the badlands much?' I asked him.

'You're acting like it's another world out here. We are all the same, mate.' Kept ploughing through the information.

I couldn't focus. Kept pushing my thigh against his. Eventually he got up. Announced he had to go.

'So how you getting back to your palace in the east?' A coy look on my face.

'I live in a one-bedroom.' Deadpan voice.

'You riding your dressage pony back home?'

'It's an Audi,' he said.

'Stop it,' I said, elongating the vowels. Stooop iiit. Tapping him on the shoulder. Holding my hand there, squeezing his toned blades.

Frown on his face. Picked my hand off his shoulder. Walked out of the meeting room. Left some work-sheets there, with his business name on it. As soon as he left, opened my gay online sex app. Found Trainer Bob's profile. Had a link to his website. Checked out the rough-headed hard-bodied prawns that he had done portraits of. Guys with weak eyes, not knowing how to stand. Guys unsure where to hold their hands. Basic bitches with overly worked pecs that had stumbled into a studio with a fresh haircut.

MALUGA PASSIVE PARK

Went for a walk, ended up at a park toilet block. Everything boarded up. Planks of wood fastened to the entrances, fist-sized iron bolts. Wood faded and peeled, that too-bright sun. Humid days made wood warp. Graffiti tags all over it. 'Antisocial activity,' said local council in one of the suburban rags. Nothing antisocial about it. That block brought people together. Truckers and office managers. Shop boys and tradies. Law students and their future clients.

Men still used it but.

Men still used it, hung around. They would pull in to the car park. For a while they'd wander around the trees, get swooped by magpies. They'd do happy laps of the toilet block; seeing the entrances closed, they would sit on the closest park bench.

I sat among the trees out of sight, looking at the car park. No persons around. Just ghost gums.

A Hell Red Commodore pulled in. I stood up, brushed crackling eucalyptus leaves and dirt from my arse.

Nice Arms Pete got out of the car. Wearing the smallest Tech tracksuit pants, marle grey. His underwear line visible on the curves of his backside. A loose white T-shirt fell off his shoulders, the hemline unstitched. He walked directly into the centre of the park. Sat at a picnic table near a manmade lake.

I stood back from him. Hid. Occasionally looking at him. Seeing what he was doing.

He looked around the territory. Head turning like a robot. Sun that fell through the canopy smashing his pink skin.

A perfect line on the table is how he placed his objects. A phone, a series of receipts and a Velcro wallet full of cashola. Every now and then he would turn his head. See if anyone had arrived at the toilet block. In the trees above him was a group of crows. A big one fought off a little one.

Heard the rumble of a car running on its last legs. Back in the car park a smooth Celica pulled up. This old Mediterranean type got out. Maybe Leb, maybe Greek, maybe Italian. Looked fucked up in that kinda way that vanity does to people. Would have been in his sixties. Faded Stubbies, a black tank. Hairy limbs like a carpet. A leathery face. Cheeks that drooped. A nose that hooked over the centre of his face.

Old Woggy wandered through the car park. Noticed the Hell Red Commodore under a tree, the only part of the car park that had any shade. He stood still. Eyes up-downing muscle car.

Fags know this car, we know it in different forms. A hotted-up version with chrome wheels overtaking us on the Hume. A car with mag wheels and subwoofers blasting EDM through a ten-speaker system parked at McDonald's. We expect a young man with close-cropped hair and bulging shoulders in it and our mouths and our fangs start dripping with saliva.

Old Woggy took a path to the toilet block. Circled it looking for an entrance. Realised he couldn't get in. At the nearest picnic table, he saw Nice Arms Pete from behind. Nice Arms Pete became Broad Back Pete, with rounded shoulders, a tight fade in his hair.

When Nice Arms Pete looked up from the table, Old Woggy was a few metres in front him, slowly walking past. Their eyes connected. Their eyes broke. Nice Arms Pete looked down at his phone. Typed something into it.

Old Woggy's legs were hairy and brown. He stomped through the park, legs took him directly to the table, and sat next to Nice Arms Pete. Sitting next to each other, looking in opposite directions. Old Woggy reached over to put his hand on his bench mate's thigh meat. Wrinkled hand rested there for a bit.

I was closer now. If they turned they could have made me out near the bushes.

'You like dick sucked?' said the old man, clipped vowels, harsh from the back of his throat.

'Yes,' said Nice Arms Pete. Because 'You like dick sucked?' was appropriate banter, like 'You like this weather?'.

He bent over, head moved towards Nice Arms Pete's crotch. Old hands seemed like claws trying to pull down his own Stubbies. His mouth formed a perfect hole that crinkled around the side, a tongue that lapped like a dehydrated cat.

'I like my dick sucked – but not by you,' said Nice Arms Pete. Grabbed the old man by the back of his neck. Flung his head away. Picked up his phone, receipts and wallet and got up to move deeper into the park.

Took a few seconds for the old wog to realise what had happened. Went from a stiff shock to slumped shoulders. He sat at the park bench; a gust of air slammed him.

Looked up at the trees, how they reached and swayed like they didn't give a shit.

Old guy walked off towards the car park, head down, eyes scanning the debris just above the dirt. Identifying objects: leaves, twigs, sharpies, condoms, empty chip packets and an old steak knife.

I followed the guy that was mine.

Nice Arms Pete stood by the bank of the lake. Water at his feet. Typed something in his phone and my phone vibrated. *Still in Orng can't wait to cum home n see u. Luvlots.*

I fell back out of earshot. Made a phone call to him and lit up a Fine Cut White.

'What do you mean you are going to be away for such a long time?' I asked, exhaling quick puffs.

'Listen, yeah, you know I'm moving this stuff and that I'm getting all this work done but I gotta stay with my fam in the country for a bit.' His voice breathy, over it.

'But what am I gonna do then? That's not fair. It's not fair at all. I've got nothing,' I said while looking at him.

'Listen, yeah, you've got all those extra work shifts, so just work, earn some money. I'll see you in no time, both of us moneyed up.' Nice Arms Pete stood at the edge of the lake. His hands were in his pockets, binocular eyes at the corner of the park, where the lake ended.

Moved my eyes to what he was looking at. There was a figure of a guy. He'd just walked into the park from the Gascoigne Road side. About a hundred and eighty centimetres, button-down shirt on pink skin and blue chinos just a little too tight. Arms verging on muscle but naturally solid anyway. The kinda guy that had pink nips and a bright pink dick with brown hair. Quick smart recognised him. Trainer Bob.

'Just remember. I love you lots. Gotta go now. Something came up,' said Nice Arms Pete. He hung up the phone. An as-the-crow-flies walk to Trainer Bob.

Hung my head. Didn't want to know more. Walked back to the car park. Eyes scanned the ground. Debris, rusty leaves, twigs and dirt, and then I saw the old steak knife. Picked it up. Rusted around the edges and the black plastic handle had faded almost to grey. Brushed leaves away, wiped blade on my shirt. At the car park I saw that Hell Red Commodore, under the shade of a coolibah tree.

The park with the manmade lake had trees and hills. Nice Arms Pete was on the other side of the slope. Line of sight obscured as I waited. Tapped my feet on the ground. One. Two. Three. Old steak knife hard in my hands. Old steak knife evil hard. Even if he was looking, wouldn't have seen shit.

I used to go through his phone when he stayed with me. He would be snoring in the bed. I'd find it in his jeans or on the floor. I'd turn it on and go through his apps and the pictures stored in his gallery. Nice Arms Pete had been taking body shots. In the bathroom he would place the phone on the sink, put the camera on timer, angle his body against the light and show off his beast mode. Each photo a different pose. I liked the ones where the camera was low to the ground and he would look down at you, his abs and chest a landscape, face stern like you had done wrong by him. Found that he had downloaded a gay sex app called Scruff. He'd cropped his head out of the body photos and put a picture up of his chest and abs, veins popping as he flexed his arms. He got heaps of messages but only responded to one. The profile he talked to was a headless torso. A let-go athleticism, upper abs were almost visible, but the V line was hidden under a layer of fat. Body fat about sixteen to eighteen percent. The arm that was flexing was holding a professional-looking camera. Dark black matt, numerous little buttons with a long lens. Looked like one of those cameras from the movies, the kind that was used by real photographers. The title of the image was MODELS WANTED. I read the rest of the text on the profile.

I am a part-time photographer and trainer. I am always looking for models, trying to increase my portfolio. Single.

Into muscle jocks younger than me. No Asians. No Indians. Hobbies include yoga and Thai food. In terms of models looking for more Mediterraneans and Latinos.

Trainer Bob's profile. I imagined cold studio walls in white with blond lights shining down on Nice Arms Pete. His oiled-up body. His limbs in a series of poses as the shutter snapped. The hot part of my head was firing up. My breathing was short and shallow. This border between two lines, getting off and the line of anger. I read some of the messages and that's how I realised that Nice Arms Pete was meeting Trainer Bob at Maluga Passive Park.

While I was in the car park I went to the Hell Red Commodore. Took the rusty knife and stabbed one of the tyres. The knife was raw, took a bunch of times to get in there. Repeated the gesture. Held it overhand. Held it underhand. Found a hiding spot just near the car park and waited.

Sometime later Nice Arms Pete came over one of the little hills. Kept on adjusting his underwear. Tying the drawstring on his tracksuit pants. Footsteps crushed leaves. Near the park the highway roared with trucks and semis.

Nice Arms Pete got to the Commodore. The sun shone onto parts of the car and he cursed himself for not putting up the reflective windscreen visor. A bird had shat on the bonnet. He got his keys out his pocket, ready to open the door. Dropped the keys when he saw what was waiting for him. The many metal keys landing on the asphalt sounded like the beginning of a song.

'FARK HIM!' His eyes ricocheted side to side. 'THAT OLD WOG!' Voice was loud. A terrier across the street started yapping. He bent over to pick up his keys and next to them was the old steak knife. He picked it up, strangling the handle of the knife with his hands, his knuckles going white. He spread his feet wide and bent his knees, held the knife out from the side of his body.

'COME AT ME!' he said to no one in the car park. He spun around, looking to go at someone. From the side a willie wagtail swooped at him. Tried slashing at it. Black-white tiny creature landed on the bonnet next to the bird shit. It puffed up. Chirped at him. And he was about to go at it. He leaned forward, ready to push off with his legs. I sent him an SMS. His phone beeped. Checked it. *Need more Syrinapx. Totes running out.*

Nice Arms Pete focused on the willie wagtail. A short body, a tail that shuddered, dirty white crest. It hopped around the bonnet of the car. It looked right at him through its side eye. Nice Arms Pete wrote a message on his phone. Sent it to me. *Nah no more. Moving other stuff now. Go 2 doctors.*

The wagtail on the bonnet. Nice Arms Pete had a phone in one hand, rusty blade in the other. The wagtail chirped, its tail spread out. He made a phone call. Told the person on the other end about his slashed tyre. He breathed. Dropped the knife to the ground.

Nice Arms Pete opened the driver's side of the car. Sat in the seat with the door open, turned on the radio. A song about driving in cars with boys. Looked over to the passenger's side. Lyrics repeated: 'Driving fast to nowhere, so so fast to nowhere.'

I waited away from the car park, in scrub. Nice Arms Pete sat in the driver's seat of the Hell Red Commodore, door open. Right foot on concrete, other foot inside the car. I watched him from my hiding place.

I remembered the time we sat in the backyard at night. Drunk from Talisker $$$cotch. I got it as a reward for moving in together. Told me about the first-ever car ride he remembered. He was next to me on the grass. Pouring himself more drink, pouring himself into me.

He was about six, standing in front of a line of tropical trees that obscured a group of trailer homes. It was humid and the smell of his mummy's BO was around. There were two policemen but Mummy was already in the back of the police car. One of them had curly red hair like a scouring pad, the other one was exactly like the red one but had brown hair. Little Arms Pete looked up at them, their size impressing him. The redheaded policeman spoke in a low gravelly voice. He had a broad thick nose, lots of freckles and an assured jawline. He bent over towards Little Arms Pete and said that he would take care of him. Little Arms Pete looked up at him and smiled with those kid's eyes that believe.

After the talk with the cops he climbed into the back seat of the police car next to his mummy. They drove down the highway and he turned around to look through the rear windshield; the cluster of mobile homes receded into the distance. He faced the front. They sped down the country road. Little eyes scanned trees, trees and trees, the bricks of a homestead gate, trees, trees, trees and the bricks of a homestead gate. His mummy next to him, her head nodding up, nodding down. Glassy eyes, two little pins. He noticed the two young policemen in the front who were taking them away, how they filled their uniforms. Their large arms struggled against their short-sleeved shirts. Their shoulder width was broader than the car seats they sat in. Mummy's thick waist, her long blonde hair a mess. The redheaded officer turned around from the front passenger seat, reached his hand over to her. His fingers moved her hair away from the front of her shirt, pulled down the scoop-neck top she was wearing. The flat hand attached to the arm squeezed the exposed breast, then jiggled it up and down. Mummy looked up and parted her hair down the middle. She displayed her teeth – a smile attempt – then her neck bent, head folding over into her chest. The policemen said something. And Little Arms Pete remembered their forced laughter from their throats.

Knew he still remembered the arm of that cop. Sunk into his mind. Nice Arms Pete called it a strong column, like it was architecture. The freckles on the arm were a sign of weakness but to a child, the width of the arm could carry the sun.

In the car park, the song about riding in cars with boys ending, Nice Arms Pete was halfway through changing his tyre. The chorus faded into the shiny red hood of the Commodore. I was still in my hiding spot, watching him.

HALDON STREET

Back-to-back work. Full days, double shifts, brain became slinky. Then time off. Two days in my room, swallowing pills, lying around. Two days horizontal. Then the pills ran out. Nice Arms Pete said that he was still in Orange, visiting family. Asked him for more pills. SMS back. *Go 2 your reg doc. Get sum pills. I b bak soon.*

Bedsheets gross. Stain pressed from body sweats and leftover snacks. Rolled over, found a tiny pile of broken Pringles. Licked my finger, pressed it onto crumbs. Brought the finger up to my eyes, put it in my mouth. Sour cream and onion flavour. Body was contorted, neck different angles to legs, never found comfort in bed. Pillow fell off the top of the bed onto the floor and collected dust balls. Reached over the side of the mattress, picked it up, brushed the dust off.

On the first day filled a jar halfway to the top with water. Sipped on it every time I needed the painkillers.

On the second day the water spilled – a clear raised map on the wooden floors.

On the third day, I slipped on the water, sprained my ankle. Hobbled to the toilet. Pain fell out of my body as I pissed. Pushed undies to the floor at the toilet bowl. Limped over to the shower. In the shower kept adjusting the heat, kept adjusting the cold. Had been renting the house for about two months, but never got used to the shower. Got angry then, list of grievances. Those taps with threadbare washers, leaking in the kitchen and bathroom. Kitchen fluoro that flickered like a strobe. Started to curse out the landlord, started cursing out the plumbing. Every person was the worst, everything was the worst. Picked up a small tube of body wash, tried squeezing it into my hand but it was empty. 'Fuck this!' Pegged the tube at the tiled wall opposite. Got out of the shower, realised I didn't have a towel.

There was a slimy trail of water from the bathroom to the bedroom. Dried myself, put on new undies, a singlet and jeans, took my keys, smokes, phone. Fucked off to the doctor's office.

•

Bus sped through Greenacre. Whipped out the phone. Checked the time, seeing if anyone had called, but zilch. Bus passed Northcote Park, group of Lebs moseyed around the fringes. Zonked like a gronk, totally in the goo goo pills smog, and I thought in an hour I could be at the chemist, a shiny packet of Syrinapx in my hands.

Lakemba Street doctors surgery looked like an old shop converted. Was on one of the main arterials of the area, outside trucks and semis passed, inside old Greeks waited while rubbing their knees, looking at other patients with an I'm-in-more-pain-than-you death stare. All my life been going there. Dr Athena, the first female doctor in the Greek community. Born in Australia, hardworking, no-frills child of the diaspora come good. Blonde bob and blue eyes, a prize among the swarthy peasants of Belmore and Lakemba. She could see through fools, compensation fakers, sickie takers and sociopaths. She saw me through childhood fevers and tonsillitis. When I was a teenling I went to her with dirty ears and flus. In my twenties she took a pen with a big pharma logo and set me on a series of meds for depression and psychosis that took me years to get off. We talked polite, a lot left unsaid, conversations like an L-plater driving into a roundabout. 'You have a kissing disease,' she said once, looking at spots around my mouth. Her gloved fingers held my lips together, my eyes had nowhere to go apart from her square-framed glasses. I couldn't see beyond her prescription lenses, couldn't see the secrets of the community.

Walked into the office, perfect air conditioner temperature. Consistent, comfortable cool air circulating, made a doctor's visit more appealing to those poor Greeks who wanted to save on electricity bills during the summer months.

Six old Greeks in the room, talking like it was a kafenio in the old country. Men all dressed up. Wore plaid button-down shirts that formed mounds around their middles. Shirts tucked into high pants. Sensible driving loafers. The women were sober, purses in laps, wearing printed blouses. Some of the men held worry beads. Rhythmic flicks a soundtrack among waiting chairs and Greek magazines. When I came in they held their string of troubles in their hands, added another blue bead to their pile of bad children and bung knees.

The receptionist recognised me immediately.

'Hello, Lambros.' Smooth voice, plain brown hair, sunless skin but looked up at me with oven eyes.

I went to speak but stuttered. Someone had used my real name. She had been with Dr Athena since the beginning. She was a kid when she started. Now had little shitlets of her own. Having kids must have softened her. 'I can get your file, but it will be about a two-hour wait,' she said. My eyes made a bullet of anger at the receptionist. Blinked down hard. The anger moved to the back of my head and settled into a lump. Shut the lids of my eyes. Exhaled a long strand of air out my nose.

'Oh, okay.' Forced breath out my body. 'I'll, um . . . sit down.'

O θεός. When I opened my eyes the receptionist looked at me, pretending, yeah, that this was all normal. Old wogs sitting in seats flanking me grabbed onto their purses just a bit tighter.

Picked a seat where I could look out the window.

The next patients came in through the door. Reception lady greeted them, pushed back single strands of mouse brown hair behind two ears decorated with little diamonds. Tiny smile that defended her against the powder blue walls of the office and old wogs prying recommendations from her.

Outside the window, Lakemba Street kept going; it wasn't resting for me or that hit of shiny pale moon. A bunch of ladies in khaki-coloured clothes and hiking jackets walked past the window. They stopped just out front and waited to cross the road.

A woman sitting next to me cursed out the strangers. I vaguely recognised her, Mina.

'Κολο Ξένι.' Said this loud enough that others in the waiting room shifted legs, wrestled with loose clothing.

Her displeasure manifested as a clicking tongue and a hissing mouth. Some of the men turned to see what was going on outside.

The women waiting to cross the road weren't from the area. One of them looked into the surgery like it was a cabinet of Greek ornaments. She wore dark chinos and a hiking jacket. Her oversized Hermès bag was a different story – a link to the eastern suburbs. Those neutral clothes, that untanned skin and a bag worth more than most cars around her was the most obvious point of difference from the locals. But on her way from a manoush bakery to a Bangladeshi grocer, her brief pause and that looking-into-a-cabinet expression was what the real difference was. She couldn't see underneath the men's shirts to the scars on their stomachs where a piston drill with broken hydraulics flew into them. She could see the women who wore blacks and reds and blues and browns, but she couldn't see how they clasped their hands in their laps, hiding pinkie fingers chopped off by a factory packing machine. She couldn't see them when the men danced their private sad dances and the women drank and laughed at their homeland's Χρίσι. Because she, Hermès woman, had cooked and eaten all their foods and seen them do their tacky synchronised public dances and she was the one who told them about their country when they drove her in a taxi.

The food tour crossed the road. The people in the waiting room turned back to themselves. Mina started asking questions.

'Ποιο παιδί είσαι εσύ;' A direct question that stiffened my spine. To her it was not out of the realm of intimacy. Thought of me as her kin, a Belmore Greek. I strangled one-word answers.

'Theodesia's.' I announced Mama's name, to put a claim on me. Said it in English to create a border between us. Looked around the room. Tried to catch anyone's eyes. Oldies in the waiting room stopped their conversation. Eyes cast down. Ears active.

'Πια κυρία.'

'She lives near the Ναος,' I said, speaking to her in English – an intimacy for parents, thought it might throw her off. Transgressing, but codes broken meant Mina could go deeper.

'Ναι μορε, σε θυμάμαι, είμαι Η Κυριά Μίνα, δασκάλα, πως πας μικρέ; σε έχουμε ξεχάσει,' Mina said, trying to make eye contact.

'Yes, I remember you too.' Picked up an old magazine. *New Weekly.* There was an article about a buxom blonde from Broome, some bumpkin broad trying her luck on the silver screen. In one pic she was getting an oversized bucket of coffee. Dark sunglasses covered her eyes, the caption read: *When not in auditions Cheyenne loves her coffee like all Aussies!* Had to reread the sentence. In another photo she wore tiny pink gym clothes and was getting out of a car. The street was lined with palms that receded into the distance. *On Sunset Boulevard Cheyenne keeps her fitness up, going four times a week to yoga and Pilates. Regulars in her class include Demi Moore!*

'Tell me, Lambraki, γιατί σταμάτησες το Ελληνικό σχολείο?' Mina put her hand on my arm. She cooed sweetly into my ear, but her niceness had the opposite effect to the one she intended.

'Συγνώμη, πρέπει να πάω τώρα,' I said. Folded the magazine into itself. Pushed it straight into the rack, scrunched into the other rags. The rustling distressed the herd of Greeks, a bunch of cows getting ready for a storm.

Stood up. Announced to the receptionist that I would be back in two hours. Scratched my upper temple. Shoulders felt heavy; they contracted into my back with a whole-body shudder. Hoped to get some Syrinapx soon. Six pairs of eyes followed me out the door. Mina was the only one who didn't release a sigh.

Outside I crossed at the lights. Memories of Haldon Street were under a truck. Everything had changed. The main shopping plaza had burned down, council had put up a temporary fence – a temporary fence that had been there for a decade. Beyond chain-link was the ruins. The cafes opposite, old men in keffiyehs with coffee mud. Beak-nosed Lakemba locals speculated: 'Insurance job fo sho.' Fugees and hijabis walked past the Gaza-like ruins, concrete walls that broke into puddles of mosquito water.

Walked up the street. Approached the corner that changed me. An Awafy had opened up there. Outside sat young men. Adidas shorts, Nautica T-shirts, burned hairless limbs. They ate charcoal chicken with their hands, hunching over plates. Loud voices speaking over the top of one another. 'I got that car so I could drive, I got that car so I could lick pussy,' said one of the youths, haircut surgically clean, T-shirt the kind of white you can only get when Mama does the laundry. Wanted to sit down and talk shit with them.

The night that changed me was in my teens. The memory of this corner sat somewhere in brain folds, hidden under those crimes I did because I was bored. A Friday night after a failed tryout for one of the sports teams at school. The wet grass of the school oval made my shoes mud cakes and I walked up Haldon Street, waiting for Baba to pick me up. The coming Sunday was Father's Day, and Mama had slipped me ten bucks to buy some kind of felt-leather dad present. Never usually carried that much dollars.

Was waiting on the corner, two guys were walking up the street on the other side. Sensed the two boys the way a chicken senses a fox.

They crossed the street; soon they'd be walking in front of me.

Put my back against the brick wall. Prevented any of them coming from behind me, a defensive move Baba taught. Felt the cold through thin blue nylon shorts. As they approached I looked down, trying not to make eye contact. Side-eye view: a blur of bright sweatpants, kicks nicer than mine, they took a wide girth. Walked past me in silence.

They reached the corner of the street, ready to cross. One of them spun around to look at me and the other followed. He had a broad flat nose and was wearing running gear. His skin was a poor dark rum.

'You couldn't help us two out?' said the one I remembered. He had big almond-shaped eyes, glossy brown. His voice went up at the end.

I improved my posture. The tone in the guy's voice had a caramel texture to it. Breathing became lighter, felt my face becoming much redder. They were walking towards me with a swagger.

Pushed my chest up, did a read of the one that was doing the talking.

'First, could you tell us the time,' said Dark Rum. I lifted a sleeve to show a silver watch.

'It's nine o'clock,' I said.

'That's a nice watch,' said Dark Rum. He looked me up and down. His mouth was tight. Just under his bottom lip sat anger, ready to erupt.

'What are you guys doing at the moment?' I asked. Dark Rum just a bit older than me; Lakemba Street light wasn't generous enough to get a make on him. Pretty shitty skin. Oily forehead, dry cheeks and already had laugh lines and frown lines all over his face. The other one was younger, a scumbag Aussie, a dirtbag colonial. Sturdy legs with red stubble and a rat's tail he'd been growing from birth.

'We were kind of looking for something to do,' said Dark Rum.

Scumbag Rat's Tail let out a laugh. A high femme laugh.

The night air was cold, the street writhed, the street wriggled, still wet from the previous rain. When that scumbag Aussie laughed, it changed the distance between us. Only one or two feet away but I could feel their breath, noticed how their trackpants fit around their waists. Their fingers were calloused with dirt underneath. I realised they wanted to unwrap me.

Nothing else.

Walked towards them, they parted and let me through. Arms hung limp down my sides and my hands brushed against their crotches. Went round the corner. Eyes making paths in the dark, ears listening for footsteps behind. Turned into a small laneway where trucks went down to do deliveries. Walked down the laneway and then ducked into the back car park of one of the smaller shops. There was an outdoor toilet, the shittiest shit shack. Single brick. Multiple paint colours. A tin roof and a chain to pull to flush the toilet.

Stood waiting inside for them. Two legs close together just fit in between the toilet bowl and the wall. Heard the two footsteps and they appeared at the door. Dark Rum took off his shirt. Compass and pen ink tattoos. He took two or three steps into the shit shack. I put my fingers on the tattoos, looked at the thin wisps of dark fluff just under his chin, assumed he got his pen ink tatts in JJs, probably Cobham. One of them was the number 2192. Scumbag Rat's Tail pulled down his pants a bit. He stood outside, pulling at himself while me and the other one went at it.

•

The Dr Athena appointment was far away so I kept walking along Haldon Street.

Ended up in front of a shop that sold Islamic men's garbs. All different kinds, grey, white and blue. Lined up on a rack on the pavement. Some of them just beyond the ankle, others stopped at the thigh. Liked the collared ones most. Touched the thin cotton, squeezing the material. The shopkeeper, a middle-aged hijabi, greeted me in Arabic. I nodded. Kept walking, head down, cheeks pinking with shame.

Past the crossing at Haldon Street, past Leb supermarkets, past sweet pastry shops, was a little plaza. When I was a teenling it had a butcher, a mixed business, a money transfer shop, an old tailor and a barber shop. When I saw it, it had gone from polite businesses in a plaza to a bazaar of bargain daily things.

All the shops I remembered had gone, apart from the mixed business. And that had changed heaps. Trestle tables were outside. Fruits like pomegranates, bananas, apples, oranges and watermelon. Other tables stacked with rows of jars filled with crimson pickles. Repetition of labels, reminded me of the rows of pills in the meds closet at work. The hunger for Syrinapx hit me. Caused a film of sweat. Sat on the bench in the middle of the plaza.

One of the shops, a juice bar run by Wahhabis. Long robes. Some were just sitting in there, hard to tell who ran the place. Outside the shop, card tables stacked with health tablets and teas. Walked in, asked for a coffee.

A young one came up to me, was wearing Nike Shox under his collared robe. Had a velvet brown beard with ginger tips at the end. Eyes pools of brown, I almost drowned in them but the young guy just squinted. He put the group handle under the espresso machine, fiddled with it. Eyes cast down, concentrating on the black stream pouring out of the machine and the steam spout frothing milk. Gave the guy some money for the coffee, wanted to exchange some words with him, but the guy started speaking to the men around me.

Went outside, sat on the same bench again. Opposite me was a no-frills bro shop. Buckets of protein and singlets. Door open, no one was in there. Next to the shop were some stairs leading up to a gym. On the landing a black shiny bike was chained to the handrail.

I was moving the coffee cup to my mouth when I realised I knew the bike. It was Nice Arms Pete's. He'd bought it just after we moved in together. I tipped the coffee cup too far and liquid dripped over the plastic spout, ran down the front of my shirt. Put the cup down. Stretched the front part of the shirt to my mouth. Bent my head to try to lick the coffee off.

Looked up to see the juice shop Wahhabis watching me in disgust. That moment when you see your wretched self through their eyes. Dirty jeans and no dignity. Fears manifest in clothing stained. Smiled at the men, shrugged shoulders, but they didn't buy the joke. Their faces gave no hint of accommodating weakness.

Ditched the coffee. Climbed up the stairs of the gym. Stood next to the bike. Paused. Walked halfway up the next flight of stairs. My head just popped above the next landing. Could see into the gym through clear glass walls. Only two or three guys in there, recognised Nice Arms Pete from behind. He was doing arms on a machine. He pulled the cables either side of him, the weights went up and then slammed down, metal on metal. They echoed throughout the whole top level. When the sound hit me I pulled out my phone.

How fam in Orange going? I typed out on my phone. Pressed send. Nice Arms Pete stopped his flies and pulled out his phone. He tapped away quickly on it, threw it near his towel. Got the message. *Pops been getting sicker. Hope to c u soon.*

Felt heart speed up. Boom. Boom. Thin glass between us. A quick walk upstairs. Took the last of the stairs two at a time. Went to the glass door of the gym. Saw Nice Arms Pete with that curvy behind and those masterful legs. Breathed heavily. Breathed low. Puffed out from the stair climbing. Wanted to scream at him. Wanted to ask where he had been. Wanted those fair legs with translucent hair. Nice Arms Pete walked over to another guy;

the other guy was doing Romanian lifts. He was twice the width of Nice Arms Pete, had a number one buzzcut.

They were the same height. Their gym clothes almost matched. The other guy had tan olive skin. Nose was broad but with a strong Greek hook. Nice Arms Pete moved behind the other guy. He put his pelvis right into the guy's behind. Put his hands on the guy's back, the guy bent over, two round circles pressed into Nice Arms Pete's crotch. As the guy bent from the waist, pulling up the barbell, Nice Arms Pete secured his back, making sure that his partner kept it straight.

I got a hard-on watching. Looked around at the other people in the gym, to see if they responded. No one cared. Some Leb was flexing in the mirror and mirin' himself. A Viet dude worked his chicken legs on the seated weights machine. Tucked my erection away, pulled my T-shirt over it, walked back down the stairs.

At sixteen I visited the Mamaland for Christmas. Greece. The land of chaos and crisis. Mama plucked me from boiling Sydney summer. Spent two months in the small mountain village on the island of origin. A tourist-free winter. Would start days with fireplace bread then take walks around the village and the terraced olive groves. It was a dead village, many houses boarded up. The general shop closed down. The only residents were some old Greek women like my yiayia, who wore black scarves over their heads, hiding waist-length plaited grey hair. The other people who lived there were affluent Northern Europeans who kept a small home in the village. One day the phone rang. Mama spoke through tears: the child of a relative had died. We were expected to go to a funeral. When they buried the kid they put her in a wedding dress. I asked why. 'So she marry someone in heaven,' said Mama.

At an ATM just down the road, I took out some bucks and then hit the Islamic men's clothes store. Grabbed a white collared abaya that went all the way down past my ankles. The woman in the shop came to help. She spoke Arabic to me. Told her I didn't understand. She pointed out that the robe was made for bigger guys than me, the size I picked all kinds of wrong. She took my medium and gave me a small. I went to the change room and took off my dirty T-shirt. Put on the all-white abaya. Just touched the ground as I stood. The cotton rubbed against bare skin. Walked outside and the shop lady congratulated herself on knowing the sizes of her products. There was a red-and-white keffiyeh amid some scarves. Picked it up.

Went to the two-dollar shop. Bought mirrored aviator sunglasses with a faux gold frame. Walked up the road covered in garb and noticed the reverence. Men nodded at me as I walked past. Groups of youths parted so I could walk through them.

Took a strong pose just opposite the stairs in the plaza. Back reached to the sky, folded my arms in a tense knot.

After a while Nice Arms Pete came down with his olive-skinned companion. Neither of them even glanced at me. I was an extra in their film.

Through my sunglasses I looked at the other guy. Bacne on his shoulders. His singlet fell loose under his arms, revealing lats that would make a sugar glider jelly. His skin stretched over muscles and made his veins completely visible. His freshly shaved stubble showed a hint of a shadow, just like me, but his skin had that never-been-touched-by-carbon-monoxide glow.

I recognised the other guy. Telly. My Greek childhood nemesis. We were family friends of sorts. His dad suffered a form of Diaspora Schizophrenia. Would often take Telly's mum and leave Telly all by himself in Australia. He was a lone pup. That island cunning served him like an armour. In primary school Telly was constantly running, kept anxious skinny. Off the leash too. Just as likely to punch out a teacher as another kid. Lifted him over my head once for play. No chance of that now. His folks and him over on Sundays. Babas drinking whiskey Cokes. Mamas downing coffees and beers. Plates of almonds and pistachios all around our living room. We would sneak cigarettes. I would show him my music or toys and we realised that there was a gap between us.

On the landing at the top of the first flight of stairs Nice Arms Pete unchained his bike. He spoke to his companion as he descended the staircase.

'I need some cardio, yeah. I'll meet you in Belmore.' Nice Arms Pete lifted the bike with one arm. He walked down the stairs, got on his bike and rode away.

Telly walked to the car park, got into his Hell Red Commodore.

I bought a second-hand T-shirt. Took off my disguise. Walked back to the doctor's. Name would be called soon. But my face skin itched from the inside. Mind stimulated by the vision. I had a shit in shitola chance of getting those pills. I walked out of the surgery without even seeing Dr Athena. She would have taken a look at my legs that couldn't stay still, my sweaty brow, then asked me to leave.

BURWOOD ROAD

It was one of those typical Sydney days. Started with blaring sun, ended overcast. People who'd dressed in shorts and thongs got caught out. Older people knew the deal. They wore light windcheaters. Packed emergency ponchos.

I knew the deal, knew where I sat, on a bench near the newsagency. Knew how the people saw me. Didn't know how I saw myself.

That day I went to Belmore to get my own back. See Telly. Piece of my mind. But there was an old Aussie walking down the main road of Belmore. Steady steps up the footpath – a slow dance. Step. Shuffle, shuffle. Step. Shuffle, shuffle. In each of his hands he held white plastic shopping bags. They spewed out either side of him. He was a thick cunt too, wearing a red raincoat and jean shorts. No one could overtake him. Stopped at the news-agency. Turned his head upside down to read the tabloid headlines. TEEN TERROR TRIGGER. Shook his head. Let out a 'Goddam 'em' low from his throat that ended in a rumble. Looked around the street to find someone who shared his anger. Looked at me. I squeezed my mouth, raised my eyebrows at him. Gave me a dirty. He had eyes that should have been blue but were so old they were in black and white. Tilted his head forward like I was prey. Looked at me like I did the shooting, like he'd bitten into a whole onion. *My people invented democracy! I'm Greek!* I wanted to yell at him. Maybe the old cunt had a point but. When she was mean, Mama said, 'I never should have bathed you in olive oil when you were born – you are too dark now.' When she was feeling nice she said, 'You are more handsome than Tom Cruise.' Told this to Nice Arms Pete once. He told me Tom Cruise wasn't that handsome.

Oldie kept doing step, shuffle, shuffle. Crowds of people bottlenecked behind him. Some tried to over-take but there was oncoming foot traffic. Crew-cut wog boys clutched Gucci bum bags, pointed to the old Aussie in front of them. Let out disappointed hisses through clenched teeth. He was making them late for hair appointments. Wog MILFs in Lorna Jane with hungry power walks. They sighed, were going to be late to the illegal tanning salon. Old yiayias mighty shitty. They sighed, the greengrocer would sell out of the good artichokes. Cafes had put tables and chairs on the pavement. Meant that it was even harder to overtake a slow walker, a class-five load, an oversized vehicle.

It had been a while since I had come to the main shopping strip of Belmore. The closing credits for ribbon developments in the area. Shopping centres were everywhere. Supermarkets so big you didn't have to leave them but you paid a price for being able to buy fresh pawpaws in the same place as detergent.

Belmore came up, but this wasn't my place. Bunch of new cafes had opened up. Places that made coffee with beans that had a certified ideology, even gave you non-dairy-based milk options. Deli sandwiches with hummus and Spanish meats. The Greek baker got a makeover. We had two zaharoplastia now and a Greek street food place all done up with Athenian-style graffiti. Food that fed the masses in Athens – a premium in Oz.

My Belmore had three or four takeaway food places. Some sold chicken and chips, those corner-shop hamburgers where they grilled the bread, a kebab shop with a sugary chilli sauce. Chinese. Greeks. Turks.

Freshies, broken English shop owners who'd change the prices on you depending on their mood.

My Belmore had gambling dens. Places that pretended to be coffee shops. First-wave Greek immigrants ran them. They were above the shops on the main drag. A narrow carpeted staircase up to a room with some tables in it. A gas stove for the briki. Packets of sunflower seeds, walnuts and almonds on plates. Posters of eighties pinups with thick blonde perms, high-cut leotards. Scrunched-up leg warmers against oiled limbs. Legs and arms slimy with an orange tan. The old men inside were slimy too, a different kind of shine. One that sweated too much. Greasy thick foreheads. Smoke floating around Brylcreem and fisherman's caps.

When I was a kid Mama used to send me to fetch Baba. It was about a ten-minute walk from my house, five minutes if I skipped – which I did, because I had that cheap kind of joy that only kids have. I'd look up at the steep stairs from the entrance. On the door a handwritten sign in black marker – Καφενείο του κρούκι – the name of the den. Curse words would come down the stairs as I walked up them. My vocab increased. Γαμισε το μουνι που ηρθες. Fuck the pussy you came from. Γαμισε το χριστο σου. Fuck your Christ. Γαμισε το χορio σου. Fuck your village. Πουστι μαύρο μαλακά. Nigger faggot wanker.

At the top of the stairs was a room with two tables. Three men at one table in the middle. Two men sat at a table at the side; they made coffees, watched the gamblers play and had a small Tavli board in front of them.

I'd have to go up to Baba. Tap him on the shoulder. Pairs of eyes looked at me, blue eyes annoyed, brown eyes with storms. Some eyes crossed.

'Hello, the boy, our big boy,' he would say. Kissing me on the cheeks.

'Mum says she wants you home now,' I would tell him.

'Φύγε κι άσε με.' Still giving me a hug, telling me to leave. All the men would turn around. 'My son,' he'd say to them. 'The one that is going to carry on the line.' Patting me on the back for achievements I'd never fulfil.

'You have girl, young studly?' asked Angelo. Bald. Always wore a fisherman's cap, cardigan and jeans.

'Yuk, Thio. I'm too young to have a girlfriend,' I'd say.

All the men would stop what they were doing and laugh. Some had a laugh like a roar, others were like cackling birds, some of the men sounded like the engine of an industrial train.

'Παιδί μου, έλα.' I went to Uncle Angelo and he would put me on his knees. Had a body like a VB stubby. Put his hand on my shoulder, ran his finger up and then down the back of my neck. All the men were watching us.

'Καμάρι, γλυκό μου. Don't get married. Women are not the useful.' Aware that he was speaking to me and a room full of married men.

'Don't listen to him,' my dad said in English. 'He has been married three times.'

'That's why I know what I'm talking about,' said Uncle Angelo. Who wasn't my uncle or that much of a husband.

'Well. Your wife wants you to come home right now,' I said to my dad. I jumped off Uncle Angelo and tugged at Baba's sleeve.

'Go home. Tell her I'm coming.' He shooed me away and I hit his hand playfully.

'She said not to leave until you come with me.'

'Go over there. Wait till this round is done.' He motioned to the corner.

I went over and sat on a hessian carpet. Leaned against the wall. Panelled in a laminate supposed to look like wood. The den filled up with smoke. Men's hands dipped into the nuts, they chewed three or four nuts at a time, cheeks expanding. My dad threw down all his cards. Told them all to fuck off. Walked home with me. Stumbling from the ouzo. Angry from the coffee.

That was my Belmore. Belmore now? That old cafe of crooks still there. On one side was a Korean barbecue joint. On the other side was the Greek street food place.

I stood at the entrance to the stairs of the gambling den. Looked at the Koreans, looked at the young Greeks. Sound coming down the stairs, cursing and spitting. Faint smoke.

A group of hipsters was walking down the foot-path towards me. As they passed each shop they looked in. Anthropologist gaze over κουραβιέδες in the ζαχορόπλαστιο. Looked in at the Chinese couple running the newsagency. Examined young Greeks drinking Nescafé frappés. The hipsters wore high-waisted jeans. Distressed denim. Washed and faded collared shirts, buttons done all the way up. Their clothes made me realise that being a hipster meant paying a lot to look poor. Must have been a Belmore write-up on the internet. *Hidden Ethnic Gem: from Greece to Korea in a single bound. Just half an hour from the city!* My tribalism shot up. Sydney tribalism. The kind that kept us rioting on beaches. The kind that threw shade at outsiders coming in to gawk at the hood. The kind that threw eggs at people as we drove past them.

Stared at the group of guys. One of them met my eyes. The next met my eyes. I kept looking, gaze turned steely. Felt dripping flames go from the front of my head, run across my scalp to the back of my neck. They all stopped talking. All looked down. All slid into the Korean barbecue. None of them stopping to look around, none of them stopping to stare at strangers and frame photos for Instagram.

The invaders infuriated. But my own kind was the one I wanted to attack. Telly. Walked down a few shops. Stood on the doorstep of the Cafe of Crooks. Heard the swearing coming from up the stairs, their voices came into me. Swearing became me. Walked up the stairs. Sat down just before the entrance. Recharged my batteries with the swearing of old wog men.

They bitched and gossiped. Complained about the troika chokehold. Merkel meant devil. Complained about oh, those Crisis Greeks/kids from their homeland, the same village as them, running businesses that didn't make sense.

'How can they charge eighteen dollars for gyro? On a plate?'

'Who buy watermelon feta gelato? Who, eh?'

'I worked twice as hard. And I earn less money.'

'Even the Cypriots don't speak like Cypriots! Where their accent?'

Kept sitting on the stairs. Looked down into the street as I listened like a spy. People walked by. I noticed some new Greeks. Their skin was clearer. More energy. Western Euro sensibility with a folk edge. Women had sunglasses in their hair. Boys had earrings, but didn't look like petty gangsters even with a limited wardrobe – botsides, we called them. No botsides in the Neo Euro.

Sat there for about an hour, criss-cross apple sauce. It was their conversation that held me there, my whole body listening. They kept bitching. Kept gossiping. Kept complaining. Exhausting everything. They talked about people. 'So-and-so's wife went overkill with the surgery,' and then, 'Fuck that man can grow a lemon tree.'

They started talking about my father. I heard someone say his name. Asking where he had been. They called him the King of his Country with a Faggot for a Son. Intends to sell his house. Get rid of the wife.

The men weren't finished and my phone started ringing. Their voices stopped. My phone kept ringing and I had to stand up to pull the pocket out of my jeans. One of the old men yelled out, 'Μανόλη εσύ είσαι; μας έφερες τσουρα.'

Not gonna lie: packed shit. Jumped down the stairs. Two or three at a time. Lucky sports shoes with thick soles. Launched myself when I was four steps above the pavement, landed right on the footpath and I answered the phone before it went to voicemail.

'Βάκι είσαι εκεί, θα έρθεις, έλα τώρα, που είσαι, ο βαβά σου δεν είναι εδώ.' It was Mama. One long sentence. Bux-you-there-you-coming-come-now-where-you-your-Baba-not-here.

'Alright, Ma, I'm coming now. I just gotta see someone in Belmore first. I gotta talk to you about what Dad's doing.'

Headed off down Burwood Road to talk to Telly, find Nice Arms Pete. And give it to both of them. It was a letter that I wanted to deliver to them, mail it with my mouth. I dodged between the pedestrians. A yiayia with a pram that looked like a spaceship almost ran me over. 'Τρέξιμο, τρέξιμο,' she said with a smile and the thickest northern accent. The Crisis Greeks looked up from eating their Athenian street food, confused looks on their faces, not understanding why an accident would not be treated with hostility.

Hooked a right at the train station. Walked parallel to the train tracks. Went down the street, did a happy lap of the Naos. All Saints' church. From the outside it looked like a small version of the Hagia Sophia in Istanbul, if it was built in the seventies and rendered in concrete.

Underneath the church was a community hall. One night a week I used to go Greek dancing there. Learned dances that Greeks did off cliffs. When Turks attacked they'd rather die doing a dance off a cliff. Learned dances that taught us about military formation, men in a line holding each other's shoulders, kicking high. Learned mourning dances. Learned dances where we criss-crossed arms in a circle, our bodies woven together into a community. Learned the aeroplane dance, arms out, our partner that Hellenic melancholy.

And two nights a week I went to Greek school in that community hall. Religion – holy wide eyes and golden Byzantine necks. Language – male, female or object. History – four centuries under the boot of the pasha. Ancient history – democracy and paedophilia. Teachers with effective short hair. Rapping us on the knuckles with wooden rulers. Boys up the back sitting in class with their dicks out. Girls up the front with tissues in their bras.

Greek education in the diaspora? It's an education of humanities, it's an education of gender.

Break times sucked for me as a fourteen-year-old. Always confused by big gatherings of my people. Groups would lean against the wall of the church, girls in Canterbury Bulldogs jerseys, Lolita femme hands holding Winfield Blues elegantly between two fingers. Boys running around, up and down the street. Telly was in all my classes. He sat at the back and I sat at the front and sometimes, as summer came, we would sit in the middle together. Knew him the best. He was the sporty type and I followed and tried to join in. When the nights were short we played footy and when the nights were long we played soccer. Usually it was touch, but one time we played tackle on the road. Streets had less cars then and the hot day made the bitumen soft.

One time I was pretending to play with the boys. Really, all eyes were on Telly. Even back then he had a body that none of us could get. Thick legs that were tanned golden brown. Body versatile. He would play winger, hog the ball, rush and sidestep the opposite team. His back would twitch and waist would twist, arch and lean, extend an arm out for balance. When the opposite team tried grabbing him from the front, he pushed his chest out, sucked his stomach in and cradled the ball against his shoulder. He would play fullback, boys would try to get through and meet a wall of him, fall onto their arses, thud onto the black hardness of the road.

During that game Telly sidestepped a guy from the opposite team, then spun around, a sweep, a turn, the strength of a muscle car doing a doughnut. As he ran to score a goal someone yelled out, 'Didja see that? What a sick move!' Telly became the words Sick Move.

Tried playing with them that day. I would use the words 'sick move' at things I didn't know. I was on the other side of the street, no one was in front of me, Telly chucked the ball at me. I caught it, then fumbled it. Ball fell down. Bounced. Went nutmeg through my legs. And I tripped on it. Did a face plant on the ground.

'Sick move!' yelled someone at me. And they all started to laugh.

I got up. Felt my nose pulsing. Six pairs of eyes on me. Could feel the warm liquid gushing out of my nose. I couldn't smell the night. Blood, lots of it, iron smell in my nostrils. The blood was dripping onto my shirt, dripping onto the road.

'Go clean yourself up. Your sick move made you sick,' said one of the guys.

'Can't even catch,' said another.

'Nah. It's nothing,' I said. 'Let's keep playing.' And I laughed it off.

They all looked at each other and then at Telly. He shrugged. We started the game again. Boys tried heaping shit on me as we played. My shirt became messier with red.

'You are gonna lose blood and die.' They said it not out of care but as a fact.

'It's just coming out of my nose.'

I wiped the blood away with my hand and caught the ball when someone passed it to me. A teacher came out, looked at me and stopped the game. 'Κάβουρα!' she called me. 'Peter, you are running around like a κάβουρα – a demon.' We all went inside. I went to the bathroom and tried to clean myself up. The blood was a bib down the front of my shirt. The back of my hand had a long streak of burgundy. Blood had crusted under my nose and I went home that day after our meal break. Went straight into the shower so that my mama and baba wouldn't see me.

The headlights of my mind revved up. Broom. Broom. Broom. Gear went into fifth. Was walking straight to his house, Telly and me two cars going down the same side of the road ready to crash.

Neo Belmore, streets paved in gold. Junkies who wore Air Max could slip on the twenty-four-carat pavement as they ran away from their dealers. Old houses I remembered weren't there anymore. Duplexes in their place. Lexuses. Jeeps. Luxe SUVs. Opposite the church now was one of those Greek private schools – All Saints' Grammar. The archdiocese must have slowly bought up all the houses and then knocked them down to build that Greek-breeding factory. The school went high, maybe five or six storeys up, and the kids inside all wore navy blue blazers with socks pulled up above their knees. They had blemish-free K–12 faces, shaded by straw hats. It was the kind of school I'd wanted to go to but my parental units couldn't afford it.

Was nearing the end of the school day. Them luxe cars were lining up to fetch their pre-teens. A woman in a golden-yellow Lexus SUV parked next to a sign that said No Parking. She wore thick-framed tortoiseshell sunglasses with pink lenses. A cream silk blouse. Her skin was absent of colour, spray or sun. Her brown hair had been dyed ash blonde and was in perfect curls around her head. Car door on the pavement side opened and a child started to climb up and into his mother's vehicle. Like climbing a mountain.

Beyond the blue blazer the kid wore, beyond the high leather car seats that the child climbed, was a real mountain, a village and terraced olive groves. Two-room houses with a fireplace and a woodfired stove and no running water till the eighties.

That mother could dye her hair any colour she wanted. She could spend two hours in the morning blow-drying a natural wave – that just-woken-up look. She could sit up high in the SUV looking down on the rest of the peasants who couldn't afford a car worth six digits, but I knew what the deal was. I knew underneath all of it were mountain legs, wide hips and a good birthing shape, were short arms, small torso and long legs that could climb olive trees and glean fields for wild greens.

'These are village legs,' I said to Telly once when we were kids. 'These are legs for chasing a bunch of goats off rocks.' I patted my shanks. 'Goats are mad. In the village, goats were like guard dogs. They would bleat every time there was a stranger or a fox around.' Told Telly information that I learned as a child. Repeated it to Telly in my own voice, making sure that the facts were accurate.

Inside, our parents were drinking their wog coffee. Outside, me and Telly climbed into the drain that ran under the end of my street.

'Goats warned if there was going to be trouble. Like, if there's a goat song there is going to be trouble,' I said. 'Anyway, see these mad chunks here . . .' I pointed to my thigh muscle that puffed like a chicken breast. 'These legs are gonna walk me everywhere. I'm gonna get a city office job, gonna go to Africa and New York. They are gonna walk me into some pretty good fucks.'

'Who's gonna give a dumb wog like you a job? The skips? You've never even met one. Never even met anyone with blue eyes,' said Telly.

'My dad's eyes are grey!' I said. Back then I waited for Scott and Charlene's wedding, how their blond heads made them look like siblings. Back then I barely met anyone whose parents were born in Australia or who spoke English at home. Cambodians, Africans, Koreans, Greeks, Serbs, Lebs and Greeks. Mainly Greeks. Fifty percent of the school was Greek.

When Telly dashed my dreams, our friendship became dodo. Tried processes to get rid of him. Tried to ignore him, which was hard to do when his parents dropped by.

Mama demanded greetings and politeness and warm Greek welcomes to the guests. I locked myself in my room and feigned sick. Goat's song bleating from my bed. Covered myself in blankets.

Telly got big freedoms early. His ba and ma went back to the village in Greece, went to die on the land that birthed them. Left Telly the house in his mid-twenties. Mama bitched about Telly's parents in a two-room dwelling, somewhere on the mountain.

On the street near the Korean church, throbbing need in nerves pumped through me, making my temples ache. Telly was onto something as a kid. Telly absorbed the television, with those blond and tanned people, lifesavers, surfers and barbecues. Telly saw the green and yellow of Australia Day magazine ads and he interpreted where we lived in Sydney: Greek delis around us, churches with their strange domes and the frankincense that burned through our houses.

Stood dead in front of Telly's house. All the trees around it jiggled in the heat. Next to the house a woman in activewear carefully opened her gate, looked up and down the street, carefully walked out.

'Watch out for his dogs,' she said to me as she rushed to her hybrid.

Looked back at the house. Still had the chain-link fence. The gate creaked when I opened it. I walked up the path. Knocked on the door. Looked at the six-foot-high wooden gate next to the house, timber colour reddish blond, hadn't turned grey – yet. Little gap beneath the gate: two sets of paws. I rang the doorbell but no one answered.

Cars went down the street, wind blew over red-tiled rooftops. I stood on the path, the tips of my fingers sparkling. Base of spine pulsing. Syrinapx part of my system. Underneath the skin on my cheeks, little earthquakes shook hidden nerves. Felt my face being torn apart. Saw dog paws move through the space under the gate. The only thing there that day were the dogs, my addiction and the Belmore of another time. Nice Arms Pete and Telly weren't there.

AUBURN ROAD

I woke up thinking I heard a fire alarm, but it turned out it was just an SMS. I was on the couch in the living room. Sleeping on my stomach. My head falling over the side, neck strained. Moved slowly when I realised I was awake. Knew that if I moved too quick this way or that I'd pull something and then I'd be in big trouble in little Birrong. Put my hand on the floor, swivelled around to put my legs on the floor.

Head hungry for Syrinapx relief. Eyes squinted down hard and I put both palms on my temple, rubbing, rub, rub, rub, led to tiny thumps, my hand rutting my head.

Checked my phone. The SMS that woke me was from Nice Arms Pete. In that MASC4MASC way told me he was going to be *Home early this arvo. Looking fwd 2 a hang.* I was cut about the Nice Arms Pete situ but I was hankering for some pills.

I use dependant rituals to find the points of time when I am ready. Some people wake in the morning as the sun tries to break through the blinds, they'll change out of their pyjamas into gym gear, get their cardio on. They turn morning sleep aromas and gym man sweat into a bathroom hygiene product cleanse. Put on a uniform that they've convinced themselves is different to the one that they put on yesterday. But in their head there's only one thing: the cigarette that they are waiting for. They will smoke it on their balcony, look over a street with peak-hour traffic, inhale monoxide deep, turn the butt into a bud in an ashtray and that's when they can cope with those days that include sayings like 'Here comes the Hump Day!' or 'How about this weather! At this time of year!'. Me, I couldn't start the day without one little pill. One shiny light blue moon. Needed that embedded S-groove in a tablet that I could follow like a song that ran along the streets of my burb, singing, 'It's gonna be alright, right, right.'

Looked on top of cupboards, ran my hands through some old receipts and mail that I hadn't opened. Turned each piece of paper into a ball when I realised that I couldn't find what I wanted.

Under the couch I found my Levi's and a sleeping bag. Picked up the jeans, turned the pockets inside out, found some old Fine Cut Whites. Threw the jeans against the wall. Picked up the sleeping bag and shook it to see what would drop out. Nothing. Left it on the floor.

Breath was becoming shorter. Didn't have any pills.

The house was a mess. Kept wrecking it more as I looked for pills.

My breath was like a strobe. Remembered that Nice Arms Pete was coming home.

I crouched on the floor. Turned myself into a ball. Pulled my hands close around my legs, pushed my head down into myself. Muscles became more and more tight. Felt my biceps keeping my legs together. My hamstrings were straining, pressing up against my calves. My body ball just toppled over. Landed on my side on the floor. Thwack. I hit the floor and I stood up. My clothes were wrinkled and stained that day. They had bits of food on them. Around the time I met Nice Arms Pete an old Ruski barman I worked with said to me, 'A man should be more handsome than a monkey.'

The first time I saw Nice Arms Pete, the days were short and shitty. They were filled with a discount-store sunlight and I breathed the nocturama. I was working at the bowlo and living in a share house. I was too old to be doing either of those things.

The bowlo had a handful of slots. Ready to go under in 3, 2, 1. No one had seen accounts in that place for years. As I poured beers for the oldie regulars, guys with white beards to their knees, they told me what the what.

Most days me and two other people in the club. Changing kegs, polishing wine glasses, spray and wiping the tables.

Meanwhile the share house I squatted in was going to shit. The bins weren't being taken out, glasses piling up in the sink, bills were stacking up on the kitchen table.

One night, fifteen minutes before closing, was the first time that I saw Nice Arms Pete. Heard the auto doors beep 'cos someone came in. Stopped cleaning the bar and went over to the flatscreen that showed security footage of the lobby.

Fifteen minutes before close. No-man's-time. The kind of people who know what they are doing will get you fifteen minutes before closing. Till is full, safe unlocked and legs are eight-hour-shift tired.

You'd think an alarm should have gone off or something. I just watched him through those security eyes.

Nike Shox – junkie attire. Flashy cheap and good for running away from your dealer who wants a debt paid. Velcro wallet – frozen child. He pulled out ID and tried using it in the sign-in machine. It didn't work. Surprise,

surprise. Getting rid of him would be easy. Junkies can't manage life administration. I could refuse him entry – no one would sign him in.

I walked over to the lobby.

I saw this: behind him the auto glass doors were open. Condensation in the park outside. Cold coming in. This guy hugged himself to keep warm. He was taller than me but looked up to see me. Overdose green eyes and speckled guns. A wheat-fed kid and I saw him swimming in billabongs near a farmhouse. Sandy hair, skin still smooth but slightly sun-aged, and you could see clean living on him. The kind of Australian I could never be. In a red coat with a musket pointed at a native.

I poured him a schooner of Bruiser. He told me he was from Orange.

'What's in Sydney for you then?' I pulled down the handle.

'I miss it by the river, but Orange is just full of oranges.'

'So why you here then?' Head fell over the glass. I put it on the bar.

'Living with my aunty. You ever been to the country?'

'Wogs only stay in Sydney or go overseas,' I said.

He covered his mouth when he laughed.

'So what are you doing here?' I asked again.

'I'm here to meet people – friends.'

He popped a ten on the counter. I took it and put the change in his palm. Held my fingers there. Skin on skin till I cut eye contact with him. Nice Arms Kid walked to the pokies.

At my crib, night, post work. Slap, slap, choke. My soundtrack was my twink flatmate getting skull fucked by some wog slut. My mattress lying on the floor, me lying on the mattress, turning heat up, no need to use blankets.

Used to take a coaster from work. Plonk coaster in the middle of my room. Broomta on my stomach just looking at it. Thirty-two hours a week like a schlub, poured beers and arranged coasters.

Used to look at my bedroom window fogging up. Heat inside, cold outside. Every time the cold moisture rose I thought of him in the cold lobby holding himself. I used to think of him, because he was the one who broke that shitty bar rhythm. Until him that life was eleven watts of nothing. His arse was two wombats fighting under a blanket and my room was filled with those empty packets that once contained sandwiches from 7-Eleven. In the foyer, when he looked at me, I thought we were going to be real love. Like that fat chick and the twink in the movie *Titanic* – but I always forgot that one of them dies. In reality I wanted to be in that film called *Riding in Cars with Boys*. I hadn't seen it, but assumed it was about handsome gay dudes with perfect stubble in a convertible.

My Nice Arms Pete obsession reached its height after he fucked me and left his train ticket on my bedroom floor. Ran down a flight of steps to catch up to him but he was halfway down the street. Saw him a few blocks down and I kept on walking behind him. Never catching up. Somehow ended up following him to where he lived and he wasn't shacked up with some Top Old Bird aunt.

He lived in a wide red-brick house with white columns and a water feature. There were two white lions guarding the gate. Lion statues couldn't protect the house from me. I walked into the front yard, looked through the windows and I saw him shacked up with a dealer.

Spent months trying to win him. Me and the dealer at the starting block. Spent months trying to play happy families, show him newlywed life and Victoria's Basement. Show him we could be the drover and his wife. Too late. Realised that people change you before you change them.

•

Mind kept needing pills. Went outside to look through my car, see if I had any in there. It was overcast. Sometimes raining but always that bright glare tinged everything with grey and blue. Asphalt shiny on the street. The neighbours' gardens looked heaps more green than I remembered. Plants loving the rain – grass on nature strips, tall and too wet to trim, in need of a Sunday lawnmowing job.

I had my head under the seat. Down there it looked like an alien grey landscape. Found a bunch of things. Heaps of those clear plastic covers from the tops of cigarette packs, looked like jellyfish swelling under the passenger seat.

Heard a rat-tat-tat on my window. Got up. A middle-aged wog chick. Dark eyes, naturally gold skin, hair chemically straight like a knife.

'Hi!' She waved her hand like a windmill and I wound down the window.

'Hello,' I said.

'My parents said there were two guys living here. And I thought OMG! Two guys? Hot! But then I realised why two guys would live together and then I thought awesome I have friends that I can go shopping with.'

I just blinked at her.

'I'm Tim Tam – that's what everyone calls me, anyway.'

Tim Tam was about a hundred and seventy-five centimetres and looked like she enjoyed Tim Tams. She had ice-cream-smooth skin and dyed black hair. She put her hands in little fists and jumped up and down. 'I am so glad you guys live in my street! It's awesome.'

There are a bunch of movies and television shows that have ruined my life. I am in a rom com and the main ho-tagonist has lost her sidepiece. Two-thirds of the way through, that's where I come in. Clumsy cute lead female is shepherded through a montage by me – an avatar, a fancy man friend. By me – the guy that gives up his own sperm to be her fashion assistant, personal trainer, psychologist.

'Who are you and what are you doing here?' I asked.

'OMG. Are you hungover from partying on Oxford Street? It. Is. A. Weekday!' Tim Tam's voice went up at the end.

I looked away, kept searching through my car. Opened the ashtray and ran my fingers all through the butts. Bent over my knees and put my hands under my own seat, felt under the accelerator pedal.

'Hey. Are you alright? Are you looking for something?' asked Tim Tam, this inflection like she was talking to a cute little puppy that she's found dunked in the toilet.

'I need my pills,' I said to her. 'I need my pills for this hangover.'

I had almost given up looking. But Tim Tam, standing there, breaking my heart, wanting to be my friend, made my eyes look down. And as I was looking down, down, down with depression, my wallet was peeking out of the side pocket of the driver's door. I snatched it out of there and opened it. There was a bunch of change and two blue pearls.

Swallow.

Silence.

I was just waiting for the painkillers to kick in. It's like a fog that comes up from the back of the spine. The fog climbs up between the shoulder blades. Moves and creates a web around the spine and then it starts swallowing your head from behind your eyes. The Sydney sunlight is less bright; you can appreciate the way the sun bears down. The currawongs sitting on fences sound almost like music instead of a funeral choir.

'I don't know how you can do that. I can't take any of my pills without water.' Her voice was like an Indian myna, defending its nest.

I opened the car door. She took a few steps back.

'I have to go now,' I said. 'I've got so much washing to do.'

'Ah ha ha ha ha ha ha ha.' She started laughing uncontrollably. 'You are so funny.'

I walked around the car and towards the gate of the cottage. Turned around just as I pulled the gate open. She was still standing in the middle of the street, gave a wave with her hand. Excited.

When I went inside I realised that I didn't want a big fight for gay marriage – all I wanted was a clean house.

The bedroom was a series of piles. Sheets. Clothes. Rubbish. I had to sort everything and all I wanted was more Syrinapx. I SMSed Nice Arms Pete to bring me some more. He replied: *Yeah. But last time. Not hooked up no more.*

After getting the house in order I had to cook something, but all I had in the fridge was some celery that had gone soggy and an onion. The cupboard had all the staples. Nutri-Grain, powdered vegetable stock, green lentils and banana-flavoured Muscle Milk Protein.

I went outside to the backyard to smoke a cigarette in the sun. The train went by. The shuddering tracks were like a soundtrack to realising that greens were sprouting in my yard. Like the ones Mama used to glean. Me and my mama. More in common than I thought. Both of us have train lines for backyards. Both of us have vanishing men and substances to lean on.

Washed a cup of lentils. Fried an onion until brown in a deep pan. Added crushed garlic for three minutes. Added some water, then the lentils. Chopped the rocket and did a fine-cut job on the celery. Put it into the simmering lentils. Turned the heat way down and added a tablespoon of Vegeta.

Just as I was turning the heat off, I heard the Hell Red Commodore pulling into my street. It was a souped-up V8, a sound that was unfamiliar to the cul-de-sac. The loudest sound we had was some of the kids using their dirt bikes. This Hell Red Commodore sounded like a bass speaker trying to clear its throat.

I was ladling the soup into shallow bowls when the door opened and slammed shut. Nice Arms Pete yelled through the house, 'Honey, I'm home.'

I didn't reply. I was putting the pot of soup in the middle of table when he came in. I looked down at the table.

'You look upset,' he said.

I turned to face him. He was bigger than I remembered. His waist was narrower. His back was more perfect. I wondered what it would be like to have command of a body like this. Knowing what to move and what to put in. He was wearing grey Tech tracksuit pants and a dark collared T-shirt. He looked clean.

A fire of want. I can't speak about it because I was limited, am limited, to describing him as something in a picture, floating across a television screen and then mirrored in my head, which became a feeling.

'I had a bad dream,' I said.

He came towards me, put his hand in his pocket and pulled out a bottle of Syrinapx.

'Maybe this will help you get over it.' He put the bottle on the table. Sat down.

'How was the trip back?' I asked.

'The country is the country. I sorted some stuff out.' He picked up a spoon and brought the soup straight to his mouth. He spat it out into the bowl.

'Too hot,' he said.

'Eat it from around the sides,' I told him and I sat down next to him.

Told him about the dream I'd had. In the dream he wasn't in the country but was working out at a gym and living with someone else. In the dream he was cruising beats in Yagoona and meeting up with guys.

He was silent after my monologue. I heard the scraping of the spoon against the bowl.

'That wasn't a dream, you fucking stalker.' He kept eating the soup, his eyes fixed forward. He would slowly scrape the edges of the bowl, collecting the coolest part of the soup, putting the spoon in front of his mouth before swallowing it. Not looking at me. I opened the bottle of pills. The pop of air the only sound. Took a couple of Syrinapx. He kept eating the soup. The sound of the scraping spoon on the edge of the bowl. The sound of him swallowing in gulps.

When I said, 'I know, Peter, I know,' his hand shot out and hit me on the cheek. The force pushed me out of the chair. My shoulder hit the floor. I rolled onto my back. Looked up at him. Crawled backwards towards the wall.

He stood up. Chair fell back. Turned to face me. Was breathing deep strong breaths. Air rushed through his nostrils. Deep into his chest. Out of his mouth. Eyes were red. Face was red. He held his arms out. Made his hands into two fists, like he was posing in a body building comp but angry. The veins on his temples ran blue across his skin. I shielded my face with my hands.

He flipped the table. Wood went bang. It settled into a spot. The pot rolled down and the bowls catapulted into the wall. Brown soup dripped down it.

I thought I could hear cars crashing into trains but it was Nice Arms Pete's seismic voice as he packed his bags. The walls of the house rumbled as I sat in the kitchen. Our cupboards were going to explode and the doors tremored. The floor had a perceptible shake. And when I heard the front door open and then the Hell Red Commodore doing a doughnut I realised that this was a magnitude nine.

I sat on the floor and didn't move.

Around fifteen minutes later the doorbell rang.

I opened it to find two cops. Both had large legs. Arms busting out of blue short-sleeved shirts. Fresh out of the bacon factory. With those belts that fit perfectly around their waists. The only difference was their colouring. One had brown hair and the other had red. Skin that looked clean. So sexy I wanted to be rude to them. Standing behind them, peering over their shoulders, was Tim Tam. She waved at me excitedly.

'Hello, sir,' said Bluey. 'We have had a report of domestic disturbance.' Had a thick drawl. The kind that fell off a surfboard. I took them inside. They sat in my living room around unpacked boxes. I asked Tim Tam to stay outside. Kept thinking about the soup pooling on the kitchen floor and I told them what Nice Arms Pete did. They told me some mumbo jumbo about court. The one that didn't talk wrote things down in a tiny notepad. Bluey said he'd have to press charges based on the statement I had given.

I walked them outside and looked at their arses. Went back to the kitchen. The brown soup dripped down the wall, puddles of it on the linoleum. Went and got a roll of paper towels to clean it up. I got on my knees in front of the mess. Remembered my mama after it happened to her. She just went and cried in her bedroom.

There was a part of me that wanted a house with this Nice Arms Pete. I thought he would come home, blond and sweaty from work. There would be pizza boxes piled in the kitchen and we would watch award-nominated television. On Sundays we would have ironic fun at the meat raffle at the old bowlo where we met.

I thought I was in love but he was a settler. Like all settlers he needed to get in, plant stuff in ground that wasn't his and then move on.

I remember in high school we learned about the art history of Australia. The people came from England, they wore lots of coats. Carried easels under their arms as they walked into untouched bush. They cut through scrub, camped out for days and then painted our rigid gums like flowing willows. Painted the dry landscape like it was the lush English countryside. Drew pictures of happy Aborigines dancing near waterholes.

It was then I decided that I needed to draw Nice Arms Pete the way he really was.

OXFORD STREET

I woke up with my phone next to my bed. Spent the morning lying around, looking at celebrity dick pics. I ranked them categorically. Marc Jacobs had the best one. But that's because he is a fashion designer and it was slightly hidden. The picture was waist-to-thigh in profile, the knob of his dick just peeping out, saying a coy hello. He was some kind of Luddite Instagram user, accidentally uploaded the photo and then deleted it. What I liked was that I got to see his meaty white hairless buttock. Looked like a round leather cushion on a couch. Imagined my head nestled in it, sometimes rimming it, other times biting it.

Kept tabs on Trainer Bob's website. It had a portrait section. Different kinds of men, plucked from the street, shed their clothes and modelled in a studio. Men who had shaved too much of their bodies. Men who had their eyebrows in long tapers, permanent surprise on their face. Men who had chicken legs and overly worked pecs.

Saw a picture of Nice Arms Pete on it. He was wearing Speedos with an Australian flag. Body was ripped. Veins popping. His white skin was oily. His face relaxed. It still let him down. Too rough. The sight of that boy, thinking he could model with that rough head, was sad enough to bring a tear to a glass eye.

There was a leg cropped out of the photo. It was brown and just shiny and could only have been Telly's. It's not a big jump, but I made the jump to Telly, Nice Arms Pete and Trainer Bob in his studio together.

After I'd had my fill of dick pics, I got up to take the rubbish out. Some of Nice Arms Pete's stuff was in there. Being the stalker that I am I went through it. There was a card with a fancy name. William Sexton, Probate Lawyer.

In my twenties I learned about these Honourable Vamp Lawyer types.

Stonewall: young men with fresh sneakers and worn-out faces, beauty tips a form of foreplay. A young me did the weeknight perch on bar stools. Ordered the cheapest middies. Arrived after sunset. Drank till close. The night-ride train to Belmore. Wake up late. Wash. Repeat.

One night, I found a dude sitting next to me on the stools. He was wearing a blue shirt, the kind he picked because he knew it would make his eyes pop. Had fried pink skin. Talked to me using words with big syllables, went from pink to red when I put my hand on his arse. Held a tumbler with a G&T. His hand shook as he moved it to his thin lips. Mentioned he'd been to Greece. I lied, said that I hadn't. I was a raconteur with stories of Sydney badlands. He was too young to be a barrister but was one anyway. I imagined him in a white wig. Curls do not get the girls. Might get the boys, the tweedy boys. He was originally from the Adelaide Hills. I asked if that was a thing. Conversation lulled. Sipped drinks.

'Doesn't Adelaide have the highest proportion of serial killers?' I asked. Actually cockblocking myself. His thin lips clasped shut.

'This is the point where you take me back to your place,' I said.

Slutty bartenders shot me a look as we left the bar. I made him walk in front of me, slapped his arse and turned around to the bartenders. I rubbed my fingers together, the international sign of cashola.

We walked up to Taylor Square. Homeless people sat in circles, passing brown paper bags among themselves.

Barrister kept looking at the toothless homeless wearing tracksuit pants and flannels. Barrister kept looking at the lights, waiting for them to change, back at the toothless homeless, back at the lights. Anxious face. I said to him, 'Don't worry. I'm from the west, I'll keep you safe.' I was more scared than he was. Put my arm around him, pulled his tiny body into my chest.

As we walked past the National Art School, I said to him, 'Wish I could study art,' and I noticed how much shorter than me he was.

'What would you study?' he asked. Put his elf hands on my wrists.

'I don't like painting. I think I'd do sculptures of giant phallic objects in pink latex and then put a police siren at the head.' Fuck I was a dumb kid. Shorty Barrister looked at me, soft blue eyes, water forming around his lashes. He stopped. Grabbed me by my shoulders. Turned to face me.

'Is that sculpture . . .' He gulped. 'Is that sculpture about AIDS?'

'Sure. Why not?' I said, looking off to the side.

We kept walking. Further into Kings Cross. The buildings weren't as tall as they were in the city. We passed strip joints. Hookers and bouncers left us alone. Coloured lights lit our conversation.

We walked off the main drag, down to Elizabeth Bay. His street had old trees that were exploding with rich green leaves. We passed a twenty-metre-wide space made into a public garden, orderly shrubs, flowers in lines; the park had its own manicurist. Apartment buildings made of brown brick, different from the rendered concrete of the Western Sydney blocks. That was the first and last time I walked through that area. I realised then how money masks itself with ideas, designs and concepts. Real money doesn't show itself with Louis Vuitton bags and a Lexus. Real money is unseen, with fancy decorations, each tile style a history. Manicured parks that rotate annuals and perennials, a giant Zen pond – thwack – in the middle. Or how the buildings were money because they had 'significant historical architectural heritage', that Deco design where bricks jutted out like Lego, overhangs where ibis nested.

Me and the Hon. Shorty got to the doors of his building. Lines and geometric patterns decorated the awning.

'See, this level of symmetry and rectilinear lines represent a post-Nouveau Art Deco, with a reference to modernity and the interwar industrial landscape – but of course it was made by hand,' he said.

'I'll show you something made by hand,' I said and grabbed his wrist, moved it to my crotch.

We walked through his foyer. Sneakers squeaked on the shiny hard white floor. Got in an elevator. It was small. Could only fit two people. Burgundy carpet. Sepia mirrors on all sides. A metal grate that had to be pulled across by hand. Something keen about it. Something keen on me in there, going up to the top.

I got in with the Hon. Shorty and his cohorts. Days passed. Played phone tag with the guy. Deliberately missed a few of his calls, he wanted me more. Knew their codes. Knew their games. What I didn't read was how he was like the deep end of a public pool – fifty metres deep with a small floater of shit.

Shoehorned an invite to a city New Year's Eve party with him. I was twenty and the fireworks were taking off. It was some all-male law firm. And if the chicks were there I didn't see them. Fancy spread with seafood slices and tiny squares of pastry. Flowing mineral water and designer drugs as opposed to the shit I used to put in my body. Most of the time I stood on the balcony and when I saw them bring in a twink who swooshed and swayed, had sunglasses with red lenses and diamanté studs on the rim, I knew what was up. 'I'm from the South Coast,' said the twink. The men huddled around him, fingered his coral choker necklace. The twink tried to open his eyes all the way but they fell into slits. The suits kept getting grabbier. Grabbier. Standing around him. A Sony handycam appeared and I knew how far the rabbit hole went. I left. No one noticed.

On the stroke of midnight, New Year's Eve 1999, I was sitting in an empty train carriage, heading back to my parents' home.

In Sydney, these Honourable Vamp Lawyer types are as inevitable for a young gay man as is losing your virginity to a homeless junkie. It's just a coming-of-age ritual. I wondered if Nice Arms Pete knew how far their rabbit hole went. I checked out this William Sexton guy online. Found a picture, looked at it. Knew that his eyes hid a cheap darkness that comes from a boring life.

SOUTH-WEST CORRIDOR

From my childhood visits, I knew Telly's house. I imagined Olive-Skinned Hulk Telly and Nice Arms Pete. Both of them standing in the bedroom. Two single beds, matching powder blue blankets, lace dust protectors. Did they stand opposite each other in that room? Perhaps using a dressmaker's measuring tape around their biceps? Did Nice Arms Pete pull down his pants and display himself on the bed like I did for him?

Thought about Telly in the house, pouring himself into the rooms like a viscous mass. The two dogs surely by his side. Maybe he would pick up a dead cockroach and throw it to one of the beasts that orbited him. Jaws snapping and in a few crunches, insect shells masticated, spit chain falling to the ground. Paws, with tiny claws. If I was in that house, I would hear the tap, tap, tap against the floors.

The time I saw Telly at the gym on Haldon Street I looked at his too-clean T, my head got stuck there. I remembered his house and its backyard. There was an old shed they had in the backyard where they kept a washing machine. It had a corrugated-tin roof that jutted out in places. Inside, grey shelves were made from fence posts. Laundry powder, White King bleach, Solvol on the shelves like trophies. Thought about Telly standing shirtless in front of a sink or just in his jocks. Nice Arms Pete would speak to him, convincing him to go and do a photo shoot with him. The dogs would have been panting, breathing hot air in and out. Telly would have hung the T-shirts on a Hills Hoist like a peace flag. Maybe Nice Arms Pete would say, 'Drive me, yeah,' or, 'Come with, jump in.'

I knew the South-West Corridor. Had driven up it many times. My dreams kept filling up with that Hell Red Commodore speeding down roads and into tunnels. Passing the mute green sign: M5 – arrow pointing ahead. Car switching gears, a muffler echoing. Nice Arms Pete sitting next to lead-foot Telly. Would the silence be too much? Would Nice Arms Pete turn on the radio? There's a high wall all along the motorway that makes the landscape beyond it invisible. The concrete walls block the sound of growling mufflers from suburban backyards.

Hell Red Commodore would come out of the tunnel and they'd pass the golfing range, the BP and the Maccas. About there the motorway becomes a bridge before it hits the east. Around and underneath the bridge, manicured greens, slight inclines form hills. A fake blue lake still, gives no hint of the hundreds of golf balls beneath the surface. Maybe as they went over this, Nice Arms Pete tried to touch Telly but he thought about me and the first time I showed him that place.

Maybe after a few more tunnels, descending then coming up for air, they would emerge at Kings Cross.

RUSHCUTTERS BAY

What if Telly had trouble manoeuvring his car around those tiny Eastern Suburbs streets? That Hell Red Commodore almost sideswiping European hatchbacks. Eventually they would find parking, perhaps near the park that was adjacent to the harbour and had those mad views, and as they got out of the car they would say, 'Oh, look at the mad views.'

They would walk among trees older than Telly's house and neither of them would know – a bat would catch Nice Arms Pete's eye and he would look up, nudge Telly with his elbow and say, 'Bro, look up there – bats, bro, bats.' Their muscled limbs would turn yellow or orange from overhanging lights while a guy wearing a scoop-neck T would walk up to them and beg to suck them off. Nice Arms Pete would notice that the guy's pecs had a line between that was more like cleavage. They might ignore him or they would do their own little chortle. Ha! Ha! Ha! Snort. Maybe Nice Arms Pete might say, 'I like your blouse, bro.'

There would be a wall that separated the park from the harbour and they could take an intermission, smoke a cigarette, hoping it would dehydrate them a bit and help their muscle definition pop. While sitting and smoking and dehydrating, they would look all the way out, all the way out to the other side of the bay. One of them might say, 'I think I can see the zoo,' and then the other one would swear that he heard a gorilla howling and the first one would say, 'Don't be a dickhead, bro. Gorillas don't howl. Everyone knows that they bark.'

There were some boats off in the distance and maybe the boats had hulls that creaked or the creaks were just laughs. Who knows. Either way it probably made them paranoid that the whole of the east was laughing at them and that the whole of the east wasn't on their side.

That quiet darkness would be interrupted when a chick jogging got a look at their toned bodies and bright activewear and mistook them for straight dudes standing and stalking in Rushcutters Bay. As she drew near them the boys would be mirin' her lean body and her exercise-haggard face – the kind that didn't care about beauty, because she was privileged enough to have other shit in her life, like her new hobby of making terrariums. She probably worked out so much her own pores breathed by themselves. Telly might lift his hand to wave at her, friendly like. She would trip if she saw that hand, then accelerate. Speed up to pass them quick. Perhaps she might scream, 'Oh my god. They are waving at me! They are waving at me!' and she would be gone. A few nights later she might sit with a group of friends in their weeknight terrarium-making workshop and over a glass of oaky chardonnay she would insist that she didn't notice what race they were but one of them could have been Middle Eastern and the other some kind of squatting Slav in a tracksuit, even though she doesn't see race all she sees are bad outfits, and then she might say, 'Gee, this chardonnay is extra oaky.'

The two boy men would be alone then. Above them, the flying foxes might be fighting or fucking in the treetops. The noises would cover the park like a doona, protecting everyone under the canopy from the angry night sky and its hostile stars.

The two boy men perhaps looked at their phones, realising they might be late. They'd walk through the park, using the map on their phones to find their destination, but the high hills might make the GPS jump and skip.

Eventually they might stumble on the Art Deco apartment and one of them might say, 'This looks like the set from the movie *Titanic*.' In front of a small elevator that could only fit two people they would look at the grate they had to pull across and Nice Arms Pete might say, 'Pull that fence thing, bro.'

They would arrive at the apartment they had been invited to and when their host opened the door, they would look inside and there would be one other guest in that one-bedroom apartment. The other guy might look exactly like their host but with different colouring, in the way that social groups of gay men do or any groups do because of tribalism and fear of the other and such. Their host might have a surprised tone and say to them, 'Come in!' and really mean, 'Oh my, you are wearing tracksuits!' The boy men would walk in, look around the apartment and wonder why there were twigs in a vase and look at the framed black-and-white photos of headless torsos and compare their own bodies to the photos and think about how they had better defined lats.

Their host would then introduce them to the other guy in the apartment, the one that looked just like him but in different colouring because of gay tribalism, and then he might say, 'This is William Sexton of Boyd and Lawson,' and the boy men from Western Sydney might not understand which part of that was his name. So they'd think of him as William Sexton Boyd Lawson.

Probably they would drink beers from a microbrewery, somewhere local that brewed in small batches. Their host and William Sexton Boyd Lawson would discuss their careers and look for opportunities to make innuendo in the conversation. Example:

A: I have been working so hard!

B: Hope that's not all that's hard.

The boy men would definitely check out the bodies of the host and the other guy. They might or might not be attracted to them, but they would compare their body shapes. Proclaim them to be suit bags, people who hunch over a desk. And then the boy men of Western Sydney might feel confident enough to take off their tracksuit jackets and wait for the audible gay gasp to occur. After which things get either more playful and flirtatious or just serious and flirtatious.

Before the party wrapped up, Nice Arms Pete would try flirting with William Sexton Boyd Lawson in the only way he knew how. It's conceivable that he might put his hand on the guy's arm, but more likely Nice Arms Pete would stand up straight, pretend that his stomach was itchy, then scratch under his T-shirt, which would lift it with a casual nonchalance and an accidental *Ooops!* that would display his cum gutters and six-pack abs. It's more than probable that the other guy would look down at the exposed stomach and then immediately give Nice Arms Pete his business card. Nice Arms Pete would read the business card and realise that his name was William Sexton and that he worked at Boyd and Lawson and that he was something called a probate lawyer. And there might be another horrible innuendo-type joke like, 'So you must be a pro-masturbation lawyer!' and they'd laugh and be fabulous and put their hands on each other's biceps. And then laugh and be fabulous. Laugh. Fabulous. And Sexton would exit.

The host, who was also a part-time amateur photographer – is there any other kind? – would move his grey or beige Matt Blatt or King Furniture sofa, not couch, to make room for a makeshift studio. He might use a blank wall for a background or hang some material for nice effect. And then maybe he'd ask one of the boy men from Western Sydney to move the sofa. But then one of them would have said with their limited vocab and unpretentious way of saying things, 'Where do you want the couch?' and he would say in that dominating and correcting way, 'I don't have a couch, I have a sofa.'

The makeshift studio would be set up in the apartment. Before they knew it the boys would have their shirts off. Their host might offer them an array of Speedos with Australian flags on them to wear. The camera would be going click, click and the holder of camera would move just a bit too close, perhaps try touching one of them in the crotch area, and they would have none of it. Perhaps Nice Arms Pete would push him away or more than likely Telly might smack the camera out of the guy's hands and the camera would explode in three different parts and the boy men of Western Sydney would run out of the apartment and put on their pants in the hallway. Perhaps they are putting on their pants when the female jogger from the terrarium-making workshop is getting out of the elevator and she sees them and runs the other way.

ORPHANS CREEK

At the aged care home I threw up on a dick that I was sucking. It was the second big Aha! moment of my life. Dream Doc Darcy. That wasn't his name. It was Gilbert Martin. I called him Doc M. Or just The Doc.

I first saw him when I was moving from room to room at Park Road Aged Care. He was in the hallway looking at the noticeboard and I saw him in profile. I could tell he wasn't from the west because of his hair. It was mid-length. All the men have it cropped short here. There was a halo of light reflecting on the linoleum where he stood.

He had on a white coat and kept his stethoscope under it. Whenever I see doctors they always make it clear that they are doctors. They'll never walk around just in scrubs;

they'll always have a stethoscope visible. Or a lanyard. Everyone has got to know that they are a doctor. Why else would you spend six-plus years becoming a social retard during the best part of your youth? Status and a lanyard. They wait for you to speak. They have the final word and doctors make sure you know that they are doctors. But when I saw him standing there in the hallway I knew he wasn't like the rest of them. I could tell he was a fancy little homo. The type that has a good body and parents who never hit him. The type that went to university because it was an 'interesting' thing to do. I always get responses from those kinds of guys. Some of them are curious; they'll try to place me, figure out where I came from. Others will just want me, my arse and my dick – they'll want it so much that they'll forget to speak. Some of them think I'm a hustler planning to rob them, when really I just have a taste for a fancy boy that night. Others will show visible disgust – the way my hair was cut way too close to the side represents something kinda poor and alien to them. And most will have no desire to fuck me. They'll look me up and down like they got my number, like they read my book, and move on. But I get something. I get a response. When I walked past this guy as he was reading stuff on the noticeboard, he didn't move. He stood there. And wait – for – it – actually kept reading the noticeboard. WTF? Snob hard, I thought. Kept doing my job. My soul could taste a bitterness.

Bruno was sitting up in his bed. Bruno had smart things to say. But only if he realised no one was listening. I caught him rambling. Eyes unfocused. His head swivelling from side to side. I said hello to him.

'Why you teach someone to swim when all you want to do is drown them?' He kept looking from side to side. Hands clenching, then relaxing. The other geriatricals in the room were asleep.

'Because at least you'll have some fun before you drown,' I said.

I started changing his bedsheets. Slipped off the pillowcase, all yellowed from where his head had been.

That's when The Doc came in. I thought he was going to ignore me again. But he came right to Bruno's side. Bruno looked up when the white coat was in his vision. The doctor waited for Bruno to speak.

'Why you teach someone to swim when all you want to do is drown them?' he asked The Doc. He rubbed his smooth chin and I kept fussing around Bruno's bed, picking up scraps, dusting the nightstand. I picked up the framed picture of him and the man he called Pete. They looked fresh and ready for the rest of their lives.

Bruno's wrinkled mouth moved. 'Why you teach someone to swim when all you want to do is drown them?' His grey eyebrows were too long. He looked like one of those dogs whose hair obscured their sight.

The Doc moved in closer and got out a pen flashlight to look into the old man's eyes.

'Do you think someone is trying to drown you?' asked The Doc. It was the first time I'd heard him speak. His voice wasn't fancy. It was plain. But he didn't mumble. All his syllables hit the right mark. Didn't have that fake Aussie drawl that people who have more money than me put on.

Bruno looked at the doctor, all confused. Eyes became intense and his arms stiffened.

I jumped in.

'Hey, Bruno. It's because the skippys can only swim in waves and the wogs drown in them.' I gave him a tight jab on the shoulder. Bruno laughed. The Doc laughed. I winked at The Doc, mouthed 'Alzheimer's' to him. He nodded at me.

'You bring me my Pete again?' Bruno asked The Doc. The doctor looked at me, like I'd caught him doing something.

'No. No. I am The Doctor.' The Doc shook his head. 'Do you know where you are?' He spoke loudly and slowly.

'This old cunts' home.' Bruno was tired; his eyes trailed off. A sigh that could end the world. The Doc moved close to me. He touched my shoulder and I stopped my cleaning. He raised a hand to my ear, recommended I leave and let the old man rest. I don't remember what he said. I remember the vowels, bass-speaker deep. I remember the consonants, sharp like a hi-hat. Remember shuddering, almost hypnotised by his commands. We left the room together. Shoulder to shoulder.

'How do you know what a skip is?' I asked.

'Sorry?'

'You laughed back there, when I called Aussies skips.'

'I grew up around Greeks. Most of them were Cazzis.'

'Castellorizians are much better than the rest of the Greeks – they wouldn't use that kind of language.' I winked at him again and he got it. It was break time. I asked him if he wanted a cigarette and he said that he didn't usually smoke but would join me in the courtyard for one anyway.

I went to my locker to get my smokes. People were coming in and out of the staffroom. I heard my phone ringing. It echoed in the thin metal of the locker. Scrambled for my keys, opened the door, rummaged through the bag and found my phone. Saw that it was Ma. I answered.

'Mama, I'm at work and I am too busy to talk.'

There was a long pause on the other end of the phone. Tried to make out anything, some rustling perhaps, something else.

'Mama?' I said.

A slam and the dial tone. I could have been sad but I was too excited to meet The Doc again.

Got my smokes. Rushed to the courtyard. Had a flick in my steps. Just a kick you had to look real close to see. Stepping feet had a little bit more flair. My toes were like confetti, the tiniest sparkler spewed shards of light from my heels.

I opened the door to the courtyard, the smoko joint, the place that was really a gap between a wall and a fence. He was standing right there. He leaned on the fence, back arched, eyes to the sky. His eyes up, up, up and away. He had taken off his white coat and placed it on the chair. Wore a blue collared shirt. He had unbuttoned his top button and his second button; black hair sprouted against that white skin that could turn pink. It was tucked into his turquoise chinos held up by a brown belt. Like he saw the outfit on a shop mannequin and decided to buy the whole thing.

Turned to me when I approached. When he smiled at me it was like a firebomb. Needed aid under attack but I noticed the shape of his body. Narrow waist. Natural V back. Round arse from walking all the time. He had a good bod. But not in a muscle queen way. It was a nice body; nothing mean like ripped muscles with pecs that have been worked out too much. For sure no Celtic armband tatts.

We spoke about stuff that didn't matter. And with everything he said I tried to be a smartarse.

'Why did you and your last boyfriend break up?' he asked, fishing.

'Well, we were really different people,' I said.

The Doc looked at me, leaned his head in and his eyes became still and wet. He nodded in slow rhythm. I kept talking.

'I liked AM radio and he liked FM,' I said.

He laughed. Fifty percent of liking someone is how they laugh. It's the kind of thing that breaks or makes long-term marriages. It's the difference between a horny one-night stand and who you want to wake up next to. It's the difference between using a condom and going bareback.

Now, to make sense of the way The Doc laughed you gotta imagine something like one of the bubblers you had in your school playground. You know water is going to come out, but sometimes it's wrecked and the water goes so high and hard and hits your face and you didn't expect it – that's what his laughter was like. Unexpected. Genuine. Clean. While all your friends in the playground realise you've been had.

He asked about my favourite part of Sydney. I said there was a nice part of Carramar; it was close to the highway but there were trees and a river and a little valley. I went there once on a hot rainy day and it felt like the tropical third world. There were heaps of big dark green trees and an excessive amount of grass on nature strips, with some old abandoned houses. One street was full of old-school wog houses, with their gardens of olive and lemon trees. Deteriorating apartments were full of every kind of person on the planet and you could go into the car parks of those places and find a matt white Lexus next to a Datsun shit bomb. The sense of water was close on the south side of the railway station, but all the shops there were boarded up and the mini supermarket had a cage around the cashier. It was my favourite part of Sydney. Just down by the river – I think they call it Orphans Creek – they found a dead kid packed in a suitcase.

I offered The Doc a cigarette and he took it. Our hands touched. He said that he didn't have a lighter. I pulled out mine. Lit it. He came in close, cupped his hands around the flame even though there was no wind. Looked right into my shadow side as he drew breath from the cigarette, the fire from the lighter, my hands holding the lighter, me connected to him without touching. Lighting someone's cigarette makes you thirty-three percent more attractive.

'Where is your favourite part of Sydney?' I asked him, grateful for no pauses in our dialogue.

'Only the rich parts are nice. But they are being ruined by hipsters and metal glass apartments made for rich people.' He puffed on the cigarette, fingers aware of holding a thin nicotine dick, too much of a good boy to be a smoker.

'What's a hipster?' I asked. Knew what a hipster was.

'Well, it's kind of like they have beards and they like doing things by hand, and they wear old things and are arty,' he said.

'So it's a rich person that dresses like a poor person?' I asked, and he did the bubbler laugh again.

'But more self-conscious.'

'I am tired just listening,' I said. He laughed again. This time his laugh had a gasp of air at the end. Shock. Like he discovered something that was terra nullius.

'You are funny.'

'Really? Most people just think I'm cute.' I winked at him.

That conversation damaged me for the rest of the day. The subcontinent of my workplace was occupied by him now. My work self and my love self became closer and less partitioned. I fought for my hatred of changing sheets and wheeling the elderly around. But the hatred was gone. Work Bux and Love Bux, no longer at loggerheads.

I even greeted our Iraqi reffo cleaners with a hey and a joy step. They had lovely comfortable shoes, they wore hi-vis accents like vests on top of the collared shirts and those kind of jeans that look like G-Star knockoffs. I waved at them. Excitedly. They looked taken back.

Had a famine so bad. I was hungry for food and love. Somewhere in my day-to-day I must have implemented a policy where I left all the good things I liked out of my life. Forgot to eat. Forgot to love. Forgot to shit.

Kept up that absent brain the whole working day. Before lunch I had to organise urine-and-shit-soaked sheets into blue bags. The laundry truck was coming the next day. By then it was time to eat and smoke. Work was the thing that I did in between breaks.

There were a bunch of people in the staffroom but I kept to myself. One of the other nursing assistants said hello. I might have been paranoid but she kept too close an eye on me. Two Iraqi cleaners were sitting at a desk with Agatha, going through plans of the place. Agatha just kept looking at the plans, pointing here and there. One of the cleaners had to translate for the woman he worked with. The Doc sat in front of the computer against one of the walls. He was typing, typing, typing away. Stopped when I came in. Didn't turn to see me but resumed typing, typing, typing.

At the locker I got the PB&J sanga I'd made. Peanut butter and jam were all I had in the cupboard. Put it under the grill before I left, to make it fancier. Went to Agatha. I was aware of everyone in the room. The cleaners. Agatha. The nursing assistant and The Doc.

'Agatha,' I said loudly, 'I am going to be eating in the courtyard today. There are too many people in here.'

She stopped talking, turned around to look at me. 'You didn't need to tell me that.'

I know, I wanted to say. *But I wasn't saying it for you.*

I sat in the courtyard, crouched next to the pot plant that held all our cigarette butts. The Doc opened the door just as I was unwrapping the foil from my sandwich. I didn't look up because I knew I would have smiled and given myself away. His crotch was at the same level as my face.

'While you're down there, love . . .' he said.

'I wanted a meal, not a snack.'

He did that bubbler laugh then squatted down next to me.

'The Elvis Killer . . .' I said and held up my peanut butter and jam sandwich.

I ate my sandwich and kept looking at the ground.

'What is wrong, Lambros?' he asked. He put his hand on the back of my neck, rubbed his thumb up and down.

It was his hand on the nape of my neck. The cool air floating around the courtyard. Maybe I enjoyed the PB&J sanga just a bit too much. 'My house is on this street – it's actually a cul-de-sac – and my house is on a corner where the street bends into the dead-end part. But on one side of the house is train tracks. On the other side is some road and a tiny hill, with houses. We called it Snobs Hill. All the houses are on an incline; they have three or four SUVs in the driveway,' I said.

'Who is we?' asked The Doc.

I looked at my watch. I was only ten minutes into my break. I was looking at everything but the other person there. The courtyard would have trouble fitting more than five people standing. But I was gonna bring some issues into it, worth more than five people easy.

'Me. The boyf. The fuck buddy. The lover. Call him whatevs,' I said.

'Oh, you gotta . . . ?' The Doc took his hand away from my neck.

I turned to see him – the first time in that courtyard courtship that I was looking at him. His eyes were cast down. Chest sinking in. The crown of his head falling.

'No . . . It's kind of over now,' I said.

He looked up at me and smiled. Caught himself smiling. Then feigned concern for my plight.

'You can tell me if you like.'

'Well, I thought it was going to be Netflix and Chill but it ended up being just Netflix.' I said it in a low voice. The Doc did that bubbler laugh. There was a space where I could open a wound to him.

'Seriously, wait . . .' I looked at him, feeling a rushing need to be away from him, trapped by how tight the whole place was. Stood straight up. Nowhere to go in the courtyard. Turned around and faced away from him. Walked a few steps, then leaned my head against the door. Could feel blood pulsing through my temples. Throb. Throb. Throb. Hoping my head wouldn't open. 'It was bad, you know. He didn't know any better.' My arm dangled to the side as the cigarette burned.

Heard his feet walk towards me. Felt his arm on my shoulder. Pulled down the neckline of my shirt. He fingered the bruises Nice Arms Pete left. I turned around. Faced him. Our faces were close. His exhale was going into my breath as I breathed in.

'Here's where you should say something. About how you are different from the rest and that you are different from my ex,' I said, meant it as a cheeky joke.

He stuck his tongue down my throat. If his laugh was a bubbler, his kiss was a washing machine. Pushed his whole body against me and my back was pressed against the door. Forcing me onto my toes. My head swayed with the force of his tongue. He vice-gripped my shoulders. The tension between us too much. My brain squeezed.

I pushed him away and we were gasping for air – like we'd run a marathon. Still staring into each other's eyes. He pushed me aside, opened the courtyard door and pulled me into the building.

I followed him as he walked a few steps in front. In the hallway the cleaners were walking past, pushing a trolley, their eyes to the ground. The Doc waited in front of the fire hose closet. He opened the door. It had a big red sign, Fire Hose Reel with a white spiral, swirling into infinity. Made sure that I was looking, made sure that there was no one around. I followed him in and he shut the door.

Maybe a two-foot-square space between us and the fire hose reel. The closet was dark. Underneath the reel was a fire blanket. He grabbed me by the shoulders again. Looked deep, deep into my eyes like he knew me, like he understood me, the pain that Nice Arms Pete put me through. Then he pushed my head down. I unzipped his pants. Took his dick in my mouth and it got hard. I gagged on it. It's not really a first date until you hear that gag sound.

As he pushed himself into my mouth my peanut butter and jam sandwich pushed itself out of my stomach. I gagged a few times on his dick. My stomach was turning.

Felt my throat tickled in the wrong kind of way and I knew that my food was coming up. Just as I was about to upchuck he moved his hips and angled his body away from me. I moved my head to the side of him, so I would vomit on the floor not on his pants. I've always been considerate.

'Oh shit. Are you alright?' he asked me as he was pulling up his pants.

'I've never done that before,' I said to him,

'Well . . . guys have spewed on my dick before,' he said.

'I meant blow a guy I just met,' I lied. Tried looking up at him. 'Soz you didn't get to finish.' There was low light. He was adjusting himself. Outside we heard a bunch of footsteps on the linoleum floor. Heard Agatha giving instructions. A minute's silence in the dark of the fire reel closet. Him standing. Me kneeling. Neither of us shifted, listening to what was going on outside, me still on my knees, me waiting.

My first big Aha! moment was when I woke up and drug paraphernalia was pressed against my gooch. A sleeping bag I was using as a sack had gone AWOL from my bed and I was lying on a mattress that had so many stains it looked like leopard print. I was spread-eagled, legs twitching. My restless fingers played a counting game by themselves. Woke when I heard a train. Wooden sleepers that held metal tracks could have been shooting into my eyeballs, irises brown and ready for some more open windows. Reined my veins in. No throbbing sighs and cryptic race against myself. Both different, but replace 'glass pipes' for 'the peen of Doc' and they were quite similar Aha! moments. Both resulted in my own personal character development. And The Doc's peen pushed Nice Arms Pete onto the off ramp of my brain. There was a highway that I'd just found out about, a new one, and I was ready to go down it.

After that, I went back to my duties. I was trying to clean out the storeroom and put away the latest delivery of cleaning chemicals. Kept replaying my time with The Doc. Kept replaying old conversations I'd had with different kinds of guys I'd porked.

'It's ghetto, bro,' said a nameless trick to me once. 'Shittest suburb in Sydney. Woodville Road and the Hume cross at Carramar.' We were talking about where he grew up.

'There are some nice parts. Like the water bit and the park,' I said.

'That's where they found the dead kid in the suitcase,' he said. Later we drove to a car park and had sex in my back seat. My body felt younger. My dick overrode my mind. And I could tolerate dumb shit.

I was picking up a box of all-purpose antibacterial spray when my phone started vibrating.

I answered the call. There was a silence on the other side of the phone. Then speaking.

'Εγώ είμαι έρχομαι στη δουλειά σου φέρε μου χαπάκια,' said my mama. She was coming to get some more pills. Ended the call. Went into the staffroom.

The Doc was there, entering data into the computer. He turned around to look at me.

Breath short. Face reddening. Couldn't keep my arms still.

'Are you alright?' he asked me.

Still wanted to rub my face in the top part of his chest, where black hairs sprouted from his blue shirt.

'What's going on?'

'Gimme one sec. Need to resolve something.' I pulled out my mobile. Called my mama. Spoke to her in Greek. Asked her to wait for half an hour before she came. Kept my eyes totally on The Doc.

'You sound so sexy when you speak in Greek,' he said.

'Round Two at the Hotel de Extinguisher?' I asked him.

In the dark closet, I got on my knees. Undid his belt. Pulled his pants down. I started by blowing air on his dick, then moistening the bottom of his shaft with my lips and tongue. Worked up to putting my lips over the top part of his head and slowly running to where it just met the shaft. I repeated this, moving my neck back and forth, adjusting the pressure of my lips, using my lungs to drain air, creating a vacuum. As I did this he started to moan and I mouthed *Shhhh!* with a mouthful of dick. I kept at my task, slowly, slowly taking more of the shaft in my mouth, until I was deep throating him, holding him all inside me for ten and twenty seconds at a time. Then I put my hands down, searching the pants that were around his ankles. I found the belt loop that had the swipe attachment and plucked it off the pants with one hand and put it in my scrubs pocket. I pulled my dick out, finished him off with my mouth. He came in my mouth and I hate swallowing cum but did anyway. After we were spent we carefully exited our closet. His face was red. I walked to the courtyard for a cigarette; he went back to the staffroom.

A while later I was in the meds closet using his swipe. The rows and rows of meds and meds were lined up. I pocketed six packets. Went to the locker to get my smokes. Went to Hotel de Extinguisher and dropped his swipe in there. Ran to the front of the aged care home, waited for my mama.

I stood out of sight from the main entrance. Down the street was an empty lot filled with movie trucks. Big fat guys with tools on their belts were rushing around, picking up lights, rolling up extension cords. Apparently our hood was the Hollywood of the west. Travel shows did tours to the ethnic food districts, reality shows set tasks for the fame-hungry and dramas loved the backdrop of our suburban decay. I puffed on a cigarette. We were just like Hollywood, but only when we found dead kids in suitcases.

Mama rolled up in a taxi. She was in the back seat. I handed her three of the packets I'd swiped. No talking. The taxi drove off. Heading down the street towards the lot filled with film and TV trucks.

•

When I was finishing work I saw The Doc in the staff-room. He appeared to be looking for something. Said, 'Shit. I think I lost my swipe. This is a fireable offence.'

'Where was the last place you got undressed?' I asked. Winked at him.

He did that bubbler laugh.

MELANIE STREET

Hoping I could score some weed, use it to take the edge off the pills, I walked to Bankstown through the streets of Yagoona.

It was a trek down Auburn Road and up through the car park of the famous KFC. Once a family got a ten-piece feed from there and a young girl got salmonella poisoning so bad she ended up permanently brain damaged. Later she appeared on *A Current Affair.* Her hands wobbled as she lay in her bed under a pink blanket; her parents spoke for her directly into the camera. As bad as television about consumer advocacy is, junk food shouldn't make you impaired. Outside the KFC an emaciated guy, wearing faded black jeans and a T-shirt with the sleeves cut off, munched on a chicken leg. The seven secret herbs and spices fell onto his shirt and he gave me a stink eye.

I followed the train line down. One foot after the other. I was one guy on the street surrounded by a canyon of flats. Four to five storeys high. Everything built within the last two decades. Rendered concrete with water stains dripping from edges. Shoddily built. Put up quick. Sold off the plan and all I got from them as I walked past were some noises and pictures. Mothers yelling at unseen children. Nate Dogg on a sound system. Freshies having illegal charcoal barbecues on balconies the size of wardrobes. Clothing hung out to dry like flags. Chatter echoing. Reverbing on flat single-brick walls. The smoke of high-density living was all around me. I walked through the Grand Canyons of Yagoona on paths through parks, on the sides of the roads that didn't have pavements, my soul sharpening.

I passed two couches abandoned in front of a tall brick fence. One was a neo French Provincial three-seater, lying on its back. Its four wooden legs were pointing to the fence. The upholstery was suspiciously clean, a shiny beige material patterned with gold flowers. Next to it was a black leather two-seater, upside down. Its frame made a perfect black sandwich, an attempt at modernism.

The half-circle sign that said Marion Street Car Park guided me towards my destination. I entered a stairwell that was inside out. Usually stairwells in car parks are covered from the elements, but not this one. Any person walking up or down it was visible to passers-by and the cop cars that drove into Bankstown police station. It still didn't stop the Skaf brothers parking their white windowless van there. A yellow wall separated the stairs from the cars; there was a frame all around the stairs, giving the impression of protection.

On the top level I leaned over the railings and waited for my dealer. Down the road was the train station gym. Cars rushed by. A shirtless guy was walking into the gym. Bright pink shorts, body completely lasered of hair, muscle definition that could start a riot in a gay bar full of fuckboys and basic femmes. His arms were slightly wet, veins around his leg starting to pop. His hair was closely cropped with a razor-line part. Brown skin as smooth as a thickshake. In one hand he shook a plastic bottle filled with pre-workout and in the other he held a cup of coffee.

I could see the sun setting in the west, next to columns of smoke, rising and spreading, swallowing the whole sky. Bushfire season meant there was a smell of trees in the air. Ash rained down on cars and people used their fingers to make smiley faces on bonnets and write things like *Wash me*. My pot dealer rolled up in his white '98 Lexus. On his bonnet someone had used their finger to write in the ash: *Wogs Rule, Aussies Drool*.

BRUNKER ROAD

When I woke up I had a craving for bad food. Something about sugar and fat and what it would do for me. I ducked to the shops in pyjamas and sports shoes, bought popcorn and ice-cream. When I paid I couldn't even look at the checkout chick, I should have been buying lean meats and sweet potato and broccoli but I. Couldn't. Even.

Went back to my house. Sat on the couch and chowed down on my presents. My small-enough-for-one-person house felt big and empty. Nice Arms Pete had taken all of his stuff away. Usually there would be one of his old hoodies draped over the couch or a sock with cum stains in the corner. When I went through the washing and the cupboard all his activewear was gone. His Nike Shox gone from the bedroom. They weren't in that special place where my pillows fell off the mattress.

I wasn't gonna be a shit. A grub. No more wondering about if he had gone bush. Or if he'd gone for a drinky wink. Or gone on the Lois Lane down the Trotters.

After I'd eaten my treats, I pulled a bong and fell asleep on the couch. Full of sugar and the last of my pot. In my dreams I was riding Ionian waves and had stolen teeth from a dragon that I was going to give to The Doc. When the peak-hour trains started rushing by, I woke, full of energy and scared. Had this fear that someone was in the house and I yelled out 'Hello!', but there was no answer. Afternoon sun streamed through the windows. Got up. I walked around and checked if anyone was in the house. Looked behind doors and opened cupboards. Didn't have anyone to call. So I called Mama.

'Hey,' I said.

There was a giant pause.

'You are calling for my name day,' Mama stated. Sweet tone in her voice. She was speaking in English. Unusual.

'Why are you being so happy?' I asked.

'Of course my son will call me for my name day.'

'There are people there.' I heard the clatter of cutlery, chatter in the background She was speaking in English to show off to her friends. 'Listen, Ma, I had this dream about dragon teeth.'

There was a longer pause in the conversation. Another peak-hour train went by my house. Held the phone to my ear, went to the backyard and waited for that prophetic gift of hers.

'Oh, what, you are taking me out? How lovely! Come over later tonight,' she said. That was the deal. If she was going to use her witchy gifts, I would have to pay. Seemed legit.

My mum, my mama, my first love. She always complained I was too dark. 'Don't stay in the sun too long, you'll look like an Arab.' Explained why I always got pulled over during summer.

'You were going awfully slowly there, boy . . .' said the wog cop that pulled me over. I was still in my twenties at the time. I was on Canterbury Road. Massive trucks going past. He was standing just outside my driver's window. Shining a torch into my back seat and passenger's side. Getting a sweet view of empty frozen Coke cups.

'So you pulled me over for going too slow?' I said. Handed my licence over.

The cop was a classic ectomorph. Blue uniform compensating for short man syndrome. He looked at my licence, read every detail. Watched his eyes, sinking into their holes, brown balls looking at the photo, looking at me. Brown balls looking at the photo, looking at me.

'Mate, we've been following you all the way from Rickard Road.' Noticed his Australian drawl. One of those wogs that pretended to speak like a skip. On the fast track to sergeant.

'That's why I was going so slow,' I said. 'I knew you guys were going to pull me over.'

'Get out of the car, smartarse,' said the cop.

It had been a long time since a cop pulled me over. I'd learned to take off my baseball cap when I was driving. Learned to wear collared shirts. Even when I was half dead from shift work, going up the Hume to visit my mama.

Didn't have a collared shirt clean on my mama's name day. So I pulled into Coles Greenacre to buy one. A black collared shirt was $14.99. Cheap compared to a cop pulling me over. Also bought some man smell deodorant – the kind that smells like a fancy candle called Mykonos Beach or Ibiza Sunset. It was in a matt black tin can and was the same price as the collared shirt. Cheap compared to Mama's criticism. Used the DIY registers. Went into the toilets. Took off my wife-beater. Sprayed Mykonos Beach candle deodorant under my arms, then all over my body. Stunk out the whole place. The toilet scent of urinal yellow cake changed into stripper's dressing room getting ready for a bachelorette. I washed my face in the sink and put some water through my hair, hoping it would dry in place.

When I put my hands through my hair, I realised it was getting longer. Reminded me of when I was in year nine and Baba had gone back to Greece again. Just me and Mama in the house. She sat me down to have a life discussion. Told me that I should drop out of high school and do a hairdressing apprenticeship. She sipped on a cup of Nescafé with milk, looked at me like I was destined to fail.

Maybe I should have done that. Then I'd be able to cut my own hair. I wouldn't be in the toilets of Coles Greenacre, drops of water running down the back of my neck onto the collar of a newly bought shirt, smelling like a sales assistant from Tarocash Bankstown.

Exited Coles and drove to Mama's. Pulled into our street. There were cars all up in the guts of our driveway. A white BMW, a shit-coloured khaki Holden Kingswood and a Celica. Side mirrors on the Celica hanging off it, ready to fall. I had to park further down the street, near one of the properties that they were turning into double-storey townhouses.

Got to the door and she was waiting.

'You are late. You are just like your father,' she said.

'How so? Isn't Baba always early?' I said.

'He is. But you are like your father because you disappoint me the way he does.' She said this in English so her guests couldn't understand.

'You have people here. We can't go yet and I need to eat good.'

'Shhh. They'll be gone soon,' she said.

The kitchen was filled with a herd of strung-out Greek women, all of them wearing a form of animal print. Zebra. Leopard. Cheetah. Kitchen den on the Serengeti. Neon eyeshadow impressionist smears on their lids. Bright blue streams. Pink lakes. Blue eyeliner. Tattooed eyebrows arching like the Harbour Bridge. Pelagia, Liki and Thoula. Twenty years in Australia. Their English was still limited to 'hello' and 'no'.

Theia Thoula was the first to greet me. She stood up from the kitchen table. She had these long νταρντάνα legs and a thick waist. Long arms that reached towards me. 'Oh, you are so handsome.' Grabbed me by the shoulders. Kissed me on the cheeks. One. Two. Three. She pressed her leopard-print shirt against my new Coles collared shirt. I pushed her cigarette beak away but her hands kept touching my chest. Mama looked at me with embarrassment or maybe a joke passed between us. I remembered the time she said to me that I wasn't actually gay, just a misogynist.

Theia Liki touched me just a bit too long, said syrupy things in my ear. Too sweet. My stomach spun around. Maybe Mama was right. Somewhere in Belmore, perhaps at the ζαχαροπλαστείο where Mama got name day cakes, she'd met Liki. They realised that their husbands went to the same gambling dens. Liki was one of those types, moving mouth, sound coming out but never really saying anything. She was wearing zebra print, legs ready for bucking. The only thing that placated her was my mama's psychic readings.

On the kitchen table, the three unwise guests had turned their coffee cups upside down. Coffee mud was dripping down the inside rim. I took a bar stool and sat down just behind and to the left of my mother. The faces of the women were frozen, waiting for their future.

Pelagia was thin but not a healthy thin. Too many ten-hour shifts on the floor of a takeaway restaurant in the city. Too much taking the train home six or seven days a week to cook for a man who gave out free and easy whomps. Pelagia had stress lines on the bags under her eyes. Her skin looked like it was made of folded paper that had been put back on her face. She wore hand-sewn A-line skirts, the ones that were fashionable in the sixties. Her blouse was cheetah print. She was waiting for Mama to speak, her head bowed.

The guests held their fingers in a Trinity. Made the cross three times over their cups. One. Two. Three. Mama picked up Thoula's cup and saucer. I lit up a cigarette. A freight train went past just beyond the back fence. When it stopped my mama started talking.

'Βλέπεις εδω.' Mama pointed at the black mud pooling in the white saucer. She passed it to me. 'Τι βλεπις καμαρι?'

All the women looked at me. I kept the saucer still, so the mud wouldn't move. There were two holes in the little mud pool and two angular peaks over the top of the round holes.

'It's a cat's mask,' I said. 'It means that there is part of her that is like a cat, independent and strong, but it's just a mask that she puts up.'

'Don't tell her this; she won't pay,' said Mama.

I passed the plate back to her.

'Χαιρετίσματα κοπέλες. I am going to leave you all now,' I said to the ladies. Got up and put the stool back under the breakfast nook. Left the kitchen. As I walked off I heard Mama reading numbers in the lines of coffee streaks down the side of the cups. Told the ladies that the numbers corresponded with certain years – when all upheaval happened. Heard her say she saw aeroplanes. 'A journey, a journey for you!' She pointed out a broken house, meaning that doors and windows and children needed to be mended. Heard her telling the women to pay attention to the next half-filled moon.

The wog ladies exhausted me. It was the animal print, it was the eye colour, it was like looking right into the sun. It was their draining energy and how they respected me for nothing that I had done, just for being a man.

Went and lay down on the queen-size emerald bedspread in Mama's room. Next to her TV she kept a bunch of Greek books. Classic Greek books that every dumb Greek who thinks they are smarter than they are has in their house. There was Kazantzakis and Cavafy. In a bowl next to them was her name badge from when she'd worked in the library.

She told me about her time in the library and how the patrons saw her as a barbarian from a foreign land. She used to stand at the information counter island, her grey bob parted down the middle. A patron would go up to her – blue rinse, cardigan – and ask for a book. She would say LOUDLY AND SLOWLY, 'Hello there. Where is the latest Jackie Collins book?' And Mama would reply LOUDLY AND SLOWLY, 'You can find it over there. In the adult section.'

Above the TV was Mama's wedding portrait. She wore a rented white dress. Had a high neckline that covered her cleavage. White polyester and lace. Her hair was black and cut like a bowl around her smooth skin. Baba had a tux with wide lapels and a black moustache. Behind them was a painted arch and painted fountain. Mama wasn't smiling in the photo. Her face was expressionless. Big black eyes staring right through the photo. Baba was smiling.

When I was a kid I'd wanted to write a letter to a friend who'd pissed me off. I told my mama this. She forbade me. Told me a story that explained the wedding photo. Told me about trying to leave my father just after they got engaged. But he wrote letters to her. In some of them he used quotes from the Bible to try to woo her back. Her mouth like honey, her breasts like pomegranates, how he wanted to drink of her wine. She left him, moved in with her sisters, found joy in taking care of her nieces and nephews, served people in chicken shops, studied English.

Then the letters got bad. The worst thing you can call a good Greek woman, even the kind of Greek woman who sometimes does and doesn't believe in God, is a putana.

The letters got worse. He threatened to kill her young relatives if she didn't take him back.

I always thought that the stress came out in her legs. Mama had legs that gave out early. Too early. For twenty years she worked in one job. Did the same thing again and again. Library assistant. Putting books away, liaising with customers, talking to the Greeks, cleaning up after little shits, watching the libraries transform from quiet solitary places of study to e-info spaces of nonsense. But getting there was the problem. She would walk to the library. Wear the cheapest shoes. Feet half an hour treading on concrete and pavement. With each step her knees kept gradually turning in. It was the slightest of pronation. Some days would give her pain. She said all she needed was a good sleep for it to go away. Knees kept turning in as she walked. The pain would come back. She said it was the changing weather, she said it was those mornings when the heat was thick in the air. But the knees kept turning in. She would say that she was eating too much. 'When I fast for Lent it will be alright.' But her knees kept turning in. When she was fifty-five the doctor told her she had the knees of a ninety-year-old. She stopped working but needed to make money. Turned to her psychic gifts to pull an income stream.

I was dozing on her bed. Woke up to the herd of Greek women making noise in the hallway. Chattering. Leaning on walls. Forced laughter. I checked how wrecked I was. Crusty saliva on the side of my mouth. Wiped my face with my hand. Licked my palms. Pushed down my hair in front of the mirror.

Opened her bedroom door. Watched the three ladies lining up down the hallway. They each kissed Mama as they left. One. Two. Three. Then put fifty bucks in her hand, a tithe for her readings.

'They are peasants. Sheep herders. I tell them what they want to hear,' said Mama as they got into their cars and revved their engines. We watched them from the door. Theia Thoula yelled across the front yard at me. Waved her hoof at me, blew kisses. I think they landed on me. Needed to shower after that.

'People don't want the real truth from the cups,' I said to Mama. Reached into my pocket. Handed her a packet of Syrinapx. 'It is your name day. You wanna go eat somewhere?'

She took the packet from my hands. 'Πάμε στο my favourite place,' she said.

BRIDGE ROAD

Mama's favourite places to eat were the bistros in the clubs and RSLs. She could get a meal that she recognised, something that wasn't strange. The bains-marie were stainless steel and hygienic. Meat cooked well done. She could get a VB shandy.

We drove up the road to the Canterbury League Club. It was the home of the Bulldogs. Occasionally I saw a muscle hulk and his entourage in there. We got a parking spot on the fourth level of the car park. Took us a while to get to the entrance of the club. She shuffled. Hobbled. I hooked my arm through one of hers. In her other hand she held a wooden walking stick that my father had made for her.

'Where is Baba?' I asked.

'He go out. I dunno. Why you ask me?' Queerness in her voice. His absence not to a perfect timetable.

She signed me in. There was a young dude who greeted us. He wore the door uniform but had black leather Chucks on. He was nice to us, I thought he was pretty cute, so I was rude to him.

Slow steps. We walked through the foyer, from where you could access different parts of the club. The auditorium. Restaurants. An escalator on the side took people straight up to pokie heaven. In the middle was a landscape feature that mixed fake and real ferns, and just in front of it was a shallow pool of dark water that curved around the small hill of plants. People had been throwing coins into the water, so that it looked like the dark bed of water had small silver scales.

We sat in a booth in the brasserie. It was early evening on a Thursday night. Place was at forty percent capacity. Surprising amount of young wog families. Women about my age who'd had kids early were joined by their young sons with trendy young haircuts. The mums wore thick foundation that covered their anyway perfect skin. Little boys and girls wore sneakers that were worth over a hundred dollars. Fathers just older than me, showered and fresh, wearing G-Star, smelling of hair product and aftershave, but their rough hands and blackened nails bore the kind of dirt that you can't just wash off. A bunch of mixed Aussies there too. Grandmas and grandpas. Big fat blonde ladies with scrawny husbands. Big fat redheaded chicks with sexy husbands. Kids in thongs and singlets eating hot chips from a plate.

'We don't need menus; you know what you want, eh?' I said to Ma. I ordered us two schnitzels with chips and veg. Got a middy VB shandy for her, some scotch for me. She asked if I had been in the sun again.

'Explains why two middle-aged checkout chicks followed me around Rebel Sport,' I said, then told Mama about the dream I wanted her to interpret. 'I was on a black liquid plane. It was like water underneath but I could stand on it. It moved from under me. Kept on thinking that it could have formed mountains or just as easily turned into a whirlpool. The air around me was black and still.'

'Αλλά που ήτανε?' asked Mama.

'I told you where it was. Some black nothing place. Where nothing was. Air was still. Like being in a closet or something.'

'Πια χορα?'

'It was in the country of my arse. Ξεσκότισέ μας. I was holding these things in my hand, there were heaps of them. They were like a dragon's teeth but they weren't pretty. They were white with black bits around them, like charcoal.'

'Very black. Πολλά μαύρα στα όνειρα σου.'

'And I would wipe away the black parts and they looked like yellow teeth. Big as my fingers. For some reason I started planting them. Started putting them in the ground.'

'Και μετα?'

'I woke up screaming because I thought that someone was in the house.' That part was half true. I didn't tell her that my ice-cream and popcorn breakfast probably caused it.

Mama told me that teeth in dreams were a bad omen. Told me to be careful. If your own teeth fell out in a dream you were fucked. If you were holding big, unrecognisable animal teeth in your hands you were fucked as well.

'What happened to the Peter, with the nice arms?' She took a sip from her drink.

A little boy in expensive shoes ran past our table, chased by his wog mum. His father was sitting a few tables down from us, a tumbler of scotch next to his food, looking at his smartphone.

'Τα χαλάσαμε,' I confessed to her in Greek. Downed my liquor. Must have been mixing with the painkillers because I started feeling my pulse more; the act of breathing was making me sway.

'I knew you couldn't make it last,' she said to me. 'Oh well, that happened. Time to move on.' She was speaking in English and holding the shandy up in the air.

'Is Baba gonna sell the house from under you?'

'He has been saying that for years.' She examined the crusty surface of the schnitzel. 'He is all talk.'

Halfway through our meal we were interrupted by this young Leb chick. She yelled out my mother's name three times as she walked past. She was a tall one. Long hair that was straightened. Kept herself well. Wore a Henleys singlet and jeans but held a real Louis Vuitton bag, big enough to fit two severed heads in. Mama up-downed her suspiciously. Kept putting pieces of schnitzel in her mouth. Little crumbs were gathering on the edges of her lips.

'Oh my god! I haven't seen you since I was studying for my HSC. Remember all those cigarettes you used to give me on my breaks?' She was excited. The Leb chick looked at me. 'We used to smoke all the time together. Are you her son?' And then just kept looking dead at me, all the while talking to my mama. Told Mama that she was married with three kids. She kept looking at me. Told Mama about her job as a paralegal. She kept looking at me.

I had worms in my seat, went to get more drinks.

I walked to the bar through an obstacle course of tables, prams and baby chairs covered in food scraps.

I ordered my drink then went to the newspaper stand and picked up an old Greek newspaper. Some wog must have left it lying around. I thought Mama might be interested in it.

When I came back from the bar, the Leb chick was still being sentimental with my mama. Kept looking at me and talking to her.

'How come you never told me you had a son? You never said anything. And he is the same age as me. But so handsome.'

'He is gay.'

'But he is *so* handsome,' said the Leb chick.

'He is gay. Gay, gay, gay,' said Mama.

The Leb chick's jeans had holes in them and were probably purchased that way. Her kids were in the ball pit near the bistro. She told Mama about her property developer husband and SUV. My mama told her I worked at a nursing home.

When the Leb chick pissed off I asked my mama why she didn't tell her friend that she had a son. Mama shrugged, said, 'I have other things to talk about than you.' Mama had some good lines that day. She kept pressing me to talk about Nice Arms Pete. I relented.

'You probably cheated on him.'

Told her that he cheated on me.

'You always pick the wrong men anyway. You are like me,' she said and I shoved more chips in my mouth. Placed a handful in my mouth every time she zinged me. *Eat, eat, eat*, she had always said to me.

'I don't go out. Σπίτι μονή μου.' Whingeing about how she never left the house.

'Let's go out then,' I said to her. 'Leave your whining at home.' That painkiller and alcohol mix wearing me out.

'Πάμέ στο θεατρο,' she said.

'Alright. Let's go to the theatre.'

We went to my car. Another long shuffle. She grabbed my arm, used her walking stick. As we walked through the foyer we didn't see anyone like us. We saw young families. Fathers struggling with pre-midlife crisis obesity. Pre-teens walked with them, occasionally looking up from their iPads. We didn't see a faggy son and his crippled mama.

●

We drove up Canterbury Road, headed for the Addison Road Community Centre in Marrickville. The darkness had set in. Our trip there was a river of red brake lights. I told her about the new guy I was interested in, that I was going to meet up with him later. Told her that he came from a rich family. That he was a doctor.

'Why would someone like that be interested in you?' she asked.

At the community centre we got lucky with parking. Mama told me about the show – it sounded like some young local wogs needed the benefit of the doubt. Hoped it wouldn't be a tacky comedy. The kind of show that put a young guy in a grey wig and a dress, and had him chase a horny Greek boy around a kitchen set with a frying pan.

Took our seats in the theatre. The lights dimmed. The ten or so audience members just looked at each other. Typical Greek commie event. Disgraceful academics. Compo wogs. Stalinists. Cypriot anarchists. Show ended up being about the Greek gods coming back to the third world part of Greece. Dionysus stepped up into a raver's world, fed kids cheap eccies instead of wine. Hermes escorted a dead junkie to the next world. Us Greeks in Australia, we like to romanticise the past, make a link to the ancients and ignore the centuries of Ottoman occupation. Our bloodlines aren't pure anymore; they are as dark as our aspirations. Halfway through, the lighting board failed. They had an early intermission so all ten audience members went outside and smoked cigarettes. Me and Ma puffed on smokes, complained that the play was too sentimental. Complained that it revived a dead culture.

Drove Mama home after the show. We sat in the driveway, looking up at the house. Only the front porch light was on. Under the Aleppo pine was Baba's Kingswood. Tree and car as old as each other. One planted from seeds that he illegally sneaked through customs. One bought legally with money from the nation building projects of old Australia.

'Don't worry, he won't come outside – probably asleep.'

'If you are really lucky, he might be dead,' I said to her. She laughed. It was funny but my old Greek melancholia rustled. That world of pines and Kingswoods. It's all gone now. Those jobs and cars for life? Kaput.

'Τί?' Mama said, looked at me like I'd lost it.

'Oh, just that car, and the pine and the world that you and Baba came from. It's all gone. I'll never be able to live in a world like that.'

'Thank god,' said Mama. 'Μι το βγάζεις σαν ένα μύθος.'

'Σκατα-λαβα,' I said to her. No turning it into a myth for me.

'Oh Baki, your hair – your hair is too long.' Brushed the top of my head with her hands. I accepted this, like an accusation against me, against that romantic myth-making part of me. She offered to cook me something but I declined. Told her that I was going out. Before I left, I apologised for taking her drugs that time. I asked her if she had seen Dr Athena. She knew what I wanted, told me to wait in the car.

She came back out of the house, put a few pills in my hand. 'This will stop you from dreaming about teeth again.'

OXFORD STREET

Me and The Doc had decided to meet at a nightclub that was called after something in the Bible.

He could have taken me anywhere because I had that movie love. He could have pointed at the sky and told me it was the ocean and I would've said, 'Yes!' because I had that television kind of love. He could have pointed at a gum tree and said it was a Toyota Celica and I would have asked if they made it in V8 because I had that singing la-di-di-di-da love. I wanted to put myself at the front of the *Titanic*, him holding me from behind, our love cutting through the cold dark ocean. I should have been wary of the iceberg. Instead I wanted to see him across the room full of self-policing inhibitions and make come-fuck-me-but-I'm-vulnerable eyes.

The lockouts had hit Oxford Street hard. It was a ghost town till I got to Taylor Square. No messy chicks in halter dresses spewing in gutters. No young men wearing their good shirts and looking for a bad fight. Late-night kebab shops closed down, no tobacconists, no greasy pizza. Night owl convenience stores kept open on the backs of South-East Asian guys on 457 visas, being paid below-minimum wages.

There are people out there that work five days a week so they can go to nightclubs on weekends. During the week they pre-pack lunches of broccoli, sweet potato, lean meat. At lunchtime they eat at their desks; the walls of their cubicles are prison bars flimsy enough to be pushed over. Plastic forks scooping in unison, picking out neatly compartmentalised food servings of the right protein-to-carb ratio. After work, metal bars go clang, routines with their personal trainers. Body parts are dissected and examined – tasks offered for improvement. Don't skip leg day. Focus on building triceps to make the bi's pop. They pass people just like them in their streets or in the halls of their apartment buildings. Take a protein shake to bed with them. They sleep and wake, each day closer to the weekend, closer to single-named nightclubs.

Since churches are dead and art galleries are date places, club land is a go-to, a destination where you can't really arrive. But part of the workday–weekend pact is a promise. Be reborn under lasers coming from above the DJ booth, meet fate as you pay fifteen dollars for a beer. Love or lust is the circuit breaker, the pinnacle and resolution. Love is swallowed easily, like the spit that collects in their throats after snorting powders off toilet seats. Come Monday they wake for work, look over to the right side of their bed, where their guest pillow is under cotton sheets, makes them think that someone might be there. The silence echoes until lists interrupt. Pack lunch. Pick up dry-cleaning. Buy steel-cut oats.

On the way to work they pass the same people in the street, or in their apartment building hallways. Lives of lists until weekend relief.

Just after eleven I entered the danceteria with all those lumpen clublanders reaching, attempting Highlander status. Walked in under a large metal sign. Hulk bouncers in black suits moved metal scanners up and down my body, trying to find knives or guns. I walked into the lobby, saw a pokie room to my right. In front of me was a girl in a cubicle. She took twenty-five dollars off me. Her hair was platinum, slicked back, her lips painted matt black: semi Gucci Health Goth. I headed up the stairs to the main room. Couldn't get to the dance floor because a wall of shirtless backs blocked me. All the backs were jacked. Some had hair growing under the blades, others smooth and white, some had freckles, and all were giants to me. I lined up for a drink next to some girls. Was the first one served but the joke was on me, bartender made my drink wrong.

Took my whiskey whatever up the stairs to the balcony. The cheapest thumping techno. Handbag house a-go-go. A diva's voice dropped out slowly then returned on the rise, paralleled by the four to the floor thump-thump. Wished I had earplugs because that music was so bad it wasn't worth tinnitus. Stood at the railings of the balcony and then looked down at the canned crowd. Ogled shirtless hunks below, they congregated in clumps. Noticed a short guy dancing around a bunch of hulks. Had dark brown skin, his chest matt in that freshly waxed way. His pecs and back too big. His thick scouring-pad hair receding in patches. Almost a bird's-eye view as he twirled on the floor, his arms out in front of him, bent at the elbow, biceps flexed. The Middle Eastern guy took steps towards a clump of jacked dudes, then danced away from them.

It was Sarkis Sarkis.

I was still living at home, days of depression. Effexor intercessions to mania. A stumpy period when I hooked up with Sarkis Sarkis. Maronite Christian. Said he was a model but was actually a hairdresser. Overcompensating with too much top bulk. Had a white Porsche that he drove disgracefully around Belmore. Picked him up one night at a beat, gave him a BJ in his car, his shaved thighs gave me a rash on my face. He tried eating my arse but instead kept biting it. Didn't call him. He kept calling me. I ghosted him.

Kept looking at him on the dance floor, noticed the group of men he was trying to get the attention of. He was like a twig hanging on an old spider thread. Four of the hulks were ignoring him, and when he danced away some of them would do impressions of him. They mimicked the way he extended his arms and swung his hips. They put their hands across their faces, leaving a slit for their eyes and did a belly dance whenever he turned around. I felt protective of Sarkis Sarkis, his tacky tattoos and large gold cross.

Noticed someone dancing among the racist hulks. He was slightly skinnier, maybe the only one of the group not on the juice. He had a hairy black chest, arms maybe too small but the pinkest nips. Eros and his unerring arrows spiked my heart. The Doc down there on the dance floor. Most of the group wore too-small jeans with decorative stitching. All of them had tattoos. The Doc did not. Not a cross on his chest, not a dragon on his sleeve, no angel wings on his back. Nothing. And he was wearing his glasses, inside a club, at night.

I moved along the balcony. Got a better look at him. Went down the steps to the level he was dancing on and leaned on a pole, in his line of vision, waiting for him to see me.

His back was arching. Hips were wagging. Had his body on display, but he did it with an unconscious ease. Men around him scrapping for attention with their bodies. They had their shirts off on purpose, their fake tans slithered over their skin. He had his shirt off in a casual way, like he'd lost it somewhere. Applause all round for his shirtless nonchalance. He wore his body like the others wore underwear. Natural. Fake-tan free. Pink nips giving me a woody. Sometimes when he moved his upper torso, I could see his ribs, diagonal lines running across his body. When I looked up at his face, the lights came from up and behind, his eyes sunk into his skull and a shadow fell over his nose, made him look like a dancing skeleton. But not just him. The rest of the revellers were skeletons too.

Just as the dancing was reaching peak morbid frenzy becoming a can-not-unsee, The Doc saw me. Stopped his wiggle wiggle. Crept in my direction. He was wearing white Chucks and grey jeans. As he moved towards me his feet were turned out. Chest and back straight. He had the kind of posture that could only have come from parents who loved him. Maintained eye contact with me. Dried-out Cola, beer and vodka stuck to the soles of his shoes. The linoleum was uneven with air bubbles, ready to burst and say Get Me Out of Here! or Enjoy Amyl-Free Oxygen! Behind The Doc the podium had turrets of rotating lasers. Coloured columns shot up to the roof, went diagonally across the room, then horizontally into the crowd. Lines of glowing purple, red, blue fell across pecs and backs. The herds of clones in clumps, skulls on top of juiced bods. Sarkis Sarkis disappeared into smoke. And I stood there, arms folded, playing my role as a member of the coy polloi. Close-ups of my sheepish smile. XCUs of my iris expanding and expanding. Bam! Had to shield my eyes from a laser beam. At first I smiled, then I looked down and away. Bit my bottom lip as his cheesy twilight descended on me.

He got to me. Thrust his tongue in my mouth. Twirled it like a washing machine. My hands fell down by my side and he grabbed my shoulders, pushing himself into me.

He dragged me up to the balcony level. There were these booths that looked like holes in the wall. There were stains and rips across the vinyl seats. We sat. Wrapped our arms around each other. Washing machine twirls of tongue.

For a breather he took me downstairs to the bar. Only one of the bars was open, people were mainly buying bottles of water. Gurning as they handed over their cash. We lined up behind guys too old to have freshly inked tribal tatts. I asked him to get me a bourbon and Coke.

'Suburban and Coke was it?' said The Doc; looked at me, waiting for a response.

'No. A bourbon and Coke,' I said, only getting the joke after he'd turned around.

We got our booze. Headed to Smokers Alley. He held my hand, pulling me behind him. I let go as we went down some stairs. Put my hand in my pocket. Felt my Syrinapx in there. Didn't feel the need to take one. I grabbed him again and we were outside. The alley had galvanised metal along one side, painted in bright, almost op art geometric shapes. Concrete walls painted a charcoal colour. Kegs haphazardly around the place, people sitting on them. The lighting was yellow and fell out of floodlights; people who I thought were intimidating inside the club were boring and average out here. Under the purple lasers and lights of the club their skin was fresh; under floodlights their giant pores were covered in sweat. Eyes that seemed joyful and alert were buzzed up on amphetamines. The Doc and I sat on kegs opposite each other. I only had a few cigarettes left. I offered him one out of my packet. He took it, put it in his mouth.

I flicked my lighter and cupped the flame even though there was no wind in the alley. He moved his face and cigarette close and looked at me, deep into my shadow side.

'I used to come here when you could still smoke indoors,' I said to him.

'I used to come here when you could still fuck in the toilets,' he said.

'Did you hear about the guy that died in the toilets and the guys fucking him just kept going?' I said. It changed the tone of the conversation. He looked at me like I had asked him to show me his dick. And then he laughed.

'That's probably the best way to die.' The joke came down like a waterfall. The Doc tilted his head back and forth. And I caught it as well but I was taking pleasure in his laughter. 'Imagine the police telling his parents how he died!'

He kept laughing. The fags and hags of the smoking alley turned to look at him.

Just off to the side a group of guys huddled. All of them wore G-Star jeans. Bankstown and Liverpool Lebs. Most of them had tight collared shirts in shiny materials with contrasting piping. Their shirts stuck to their bodies, wet around their armpits and stomachs, making the fabric translucent. Their eyebrows were long thin tapers that

had been overly plucked. Only one of the guys was shirtless; he had the big puffy body of someone shooting up
T. He had a layer of falafel fat over his stomach, his pecs
were half muscle and half man boob. Some of the Leb
group looked over to see The Doc laughing. The shirtless
one moved his body, turned the wheels, positioning his
body in the line of sight of The Doc.

The Doc asked me about my day, flicked his eyes –
quick glance to the Lebbo Hulk.

There was a group of Asian guys flanking him.
Some masc, some femme. High-pitched voices, the men
comparing sneakers. Whose were fresher? The Lebs who
were just to my right told anecdotes then laughed. They
told fuck stories, each man trumping the other. Dotted
throughout the smokers, white retail fags, men in hospit-
ality with their hags. Hags saying, 'Gee, I feel so safe
here!' What they didn't know was there were straight
guys pretending in fag drag, dancing among them in the
club. Ready to pounce on drunk chicks who thought
they were making out with a gay guy.

In gay bars men play The Game; my job was to prove
that I wasn't even on the field.

'My day today?' My voice went up at the end. I recrossed
my legs, and adjusted the way I was sitting. 'Actually,
I took my mama to the Greek theatre on Addison Road.'

I didn't tell him about how we had chicken schnitzel at the leagues club first.

'Oh really?' he said. 'You go to the theatre?' He smiled slightly.

'Nup. Go to Greek Theatre. Not *My Big Fat Wogs Out of Work* shit either.'

'What was it about?'

'Kind of a Humpty Dumpty junkie magic realist thing.'

He laughed and I continued.

'If the gods came back and intervened in our shitty daily lives.'

'Oh, like John Banville?'

I nodded. Not knowing who John Banville was.

Our conversation stopped. I puffed my smoke. Looked around the alley.

'I hate coming to gay bars,' I said. 'The first question people always ask is: "What do you do?" But you must love that question.' I winked at him.

'Actually I prefer the question: "How much do you earn?"' He winked back at me.

There was someone standing directly opposite me. He moved in closer and I had to look up to see who it was.

'Bux. Remember me?' Deep vowels, voice like a strong blast of hot air.

'Sarkis. Such a long time.'

In those Effexor days I'd pick up the worst of strays. Occasionally some teen twink would follow me around Belmore. Once a kid asked me for a cigarette while playing with his dick. I asked him his age and he told me he was thirteen. Told him that was an unlucky age, gave him a cigarette, sent him on his way. Sarkis Sarkis came up to me once when I was leaning on the fence, looking over the railway tracks. I had seen him in his white Porsche driving up the main street of Belmore. He asked me for a cigarette. I gave him one. We chatted about nothing. Went for a walk to the park. He told me about his workout routine, then asked me to feel his pecs. 'Touch here,' he said, tensing his arms in front of his chest. Blammo. Blow job. Bonking. Car park. As I gave him head he kept on repeating, 'Oh . . . I luurv it,' with his thick Leb accent. 'Oh . . . I luurv it.' His breaths punctuating the syllables.

In the light of the alley, I could see that Sarkis Sarkis had finally spent a bunch of money on laser hair removal. His eyebrows had the same wide part and tapering plucked arch. He looked me up and down, then looked at The Doc, shirtless, white, black hairs on his chest and his lithe body.

'Hey, good to see you, man . . .' he said to me. Then turned to face The Doc. 'Who is your friend here?'

I watched them, saw their eyes meet.

The Doc said, 'Hello. I'm Gil.'

Sarkis Sarkis put out his hand and they shook. Kept holding eye contact. The Lebbo licked his lips.

'How do you two know each other?' Sarkis Sarkis asked, still holding the hand of The Doc. He started to scratch his nipple, then rubbed the middle of his chest. The Doc's eyes were drawn to his honking big man boobs.

'Just work,' said The Doc.

'What do you do?' asked Sarkis Sarkis, his tone flat and neutral. But The Doc didn't reply.

'He is a doctor,' I said to Sarkis Sarkis.

'Wallah.' Sarkis Sarkis's eyes turned into jewels, looked down on The Doc.

The Doc looked at me, embarrassed.

'But he isn't as socially retarded as most doctors,' I added, but it didn't matter. Sarkis Sarkis flicked his eyes over to me and then back to The Doc.

'So why is a doctor hanging out with this guy?' Sarkis Sarkis asked him, playful, attempting to dom.

The Doc needed to piss. He went to the toilet. Left me there with Sarkis Sarkis. One of the other shirtless Leb boys came over to join us. Introduced himself as Nader. Nader was tall, thick like a superman. Tapered eyebrows. A full-sleeve tatt that he had done in one sitting. The two guys talked to each other. I introduced myself to Nader.

Told the boys I was running low on smokes. Asked for a cigarette and they said they didn't have any.

The Doc came back. Sarkis Sarkis introduced Nader to The Doc. Nader's first question to him was: 'What do you do?' The Doc tried to make eye contact with me, but I looked down at the floor.

When The Doc answered Nader offered him a cigarette. Nader said that he worked in medical sales and that he travelled around a lot. No one had asked me. My cue to exit.

'Hey, I gotta run get cigs before the lockout hits,' I said to The Doc. 'Back in five.'

The two wog boys thought they had him in their claws. Playing the love game is a gamble. And you gotta be prepared to put your heart on the table. But you might lose it if you get dealt the wrong cards.

I ducked out of the club. Hit Taylor Square. Found a convenience store and paid too much for the Fine Cut Whites. The guy behind the counter was too tired to make eye contact. I eyed the condoms and lube sitting next to the sugar-free gum and discounted energy drinks. Bought a red Gatorade, smoked a cigarette on the grassy knoll at Taylor Square. A bunch of rainbow flags hung off the streetlights. The streets were filled with backpackers. Brit boys and girls who had come to Australia and become lobsters in the sun. The good kids were just hitting Marquee and the entertainment district all around Darling Harbour. My mind jumped, skidded between Mama at home and all the things that were happening there on Oxford Street.

I saw a woman around my mama's age and height. She had a perfect platinum bob, salon cut and dry. Wore all black clothing, had a kind of Health Goth grandmother aesthetic. Shoes were plastic wedges with buckle straps that went all the way to her knees. She was with two tweedy gay men. Little-dog-owning types. Laughing. Eyes optimistic. Lightning bolts in her step. A post-supper constitutional with the squad.

I got an SMS from The Doc. *Are you back yet?*

Told him where I was. Didn't know if he would come out to meet me. Next to me two guys were talking. One looked woggy, he seemed drunk. He was sitting on the grass, wearing a blazer over a multicoloured T-shirt. The guy he was talking to was standing, wore a white Bonds T-shirt, jeans and hi-tops. The woggy guy kept trying to explain that he was bisexual. He would raise both his hands and say, 'I don't usually do this with guys!' and, 'I swear I am not interested in this kind of thing usually!'

'What happened to you?' It was The Doc. I turned to face him. He had found his shirt and put it on. Had a thin film of sweat on him. He wiped his forehead by lifting up the bottom of his shirt. His hairy white stomach made me all kinds of cray.

'Came out to get smokes,' I said to him. Didn't say to him that I thought one or two Lebs were taking him home. 'They're much cheaper outside.' Didn't say that I walked off not knowing if I'd see him again that night.

'My place is just down there.' He took his keys out of his pocket and then dangled them in front of me.

'Ooooh! Shiny!' I grabbed at them.

He pulled his hand away, grabbed my arm and stuck his tongue deep into me.

We headed down Oxford Street. The streets were empty – or they might as well have been. There was just the two of us. He walked next to me. Put his arm around my waist. Pulling me into him. Two figures walking. Step by step. Deeper into the strip. When I'd left the club that night, not knowing if I'd see him again, a crisp air had made me static. Now my red jelly heart pumped blood.

His apartment was in a back street. A loft studio situation decorated with hard leather chairs and simple things. The sex was suitable but the mattress was amaze. I fell asleep. Solid eight hours. He was gone the next morning, leaving me a note. I showered and got dressed. Took my jacket and went to a coffee shop. Ordered a long black and got bored enough to check out the sex apps. I read the profiles. Compared them to ones that I saw in the west. Their words were different. Used status statements like Professional and Play as Hard as I Work. The pics were different too. More shirtless dudes. With tight bodies. Links to Instagram accounts showing these men playing as hard as they worked while standing around in their Speedos on a beach or yacht.

It was a shock to see Nice Arms Pete's profile. He was a few hundred metres away from me. Every time I refreshed he got closer and closer. Moving up in the grid of squares.

I asked for a takeaway coffee cup, poured my long black in there. Put my jacket on. Held my phone in my hand. Walked around the city. Updated the grid of profiles every time I'd moved a hundred metres or so.

At first I couldn't work out what direction he was in. Walked one way, his profile on the grid moved further away. Turned around. Walked another way. Slowly, slowly, kept getting closer to him.

I found him in a cafe on Crown Street. It was a big-windowed shabby chic affair. Had milk crates for seating, with grandma knit pillows on top. Nice Arms Pete was in the back. As soon as I saw him I stepped back from the window. Peered around. Nice Arms Pete was sitting across from a suit bag. He was holding a coffee cup, lifting it up with both hands, sometimes covering his face and giving off a coy damsel look. The suit bag opposite him looked familiar; perhaps I had seen him before, or maybe he had one of those handsome faces that everyone knew. He was showing Nice Arms Pete a bunch of paperwork. Flicking through the pages and pointing at parts of it.

What I expected was Nice Arms Pete and the familiar suit bag to be holding hands. Get that stomach punch feeling. Got nothing. The Doc tsunami had flooded my heart.

But when I got home that day I rummaged through my rubbish bin. Found the business card that Nice Arms Pete had left in my house. Image searched the name William Sexton and found one pic of him. Standing against a grey wall. No smile. Slick dark blond hair. Red tie and blue jacket. The familiar face that hid secrets. The familiar face sitting opposite Nice Arms Pete in a cafe poring over docs.

SESAME STREET

We had about seven cats in ten years. Mama was worried that the neighbours thought we ate them like the Chinese did. She named the female cats after women she learned about when she was in high school studying the ancients. Dido. Cleo. Clytie.

All the males were called Junior. Junior One. Junior Two. Junior Three.

When we got to cat number seven, we stopped with the names. Just called it Psst Psst.

Once Psst Psst was hopping on and off my mama's lap. 'I love its tail!' she said, stroking the tail that was like a black bottlebrush flower. Her index finger and thumb formed a circle and ran up and down the tail of the cat.

She was sitting on a plastic chair, smoking a Winfield Gold, sipping on Blend 43 – no milk, no sugar. Her eyes were fixed on the plants that she had cultivated under the tin roof of the veranda. I asked her why the male cats never got names.

'Because men are all useless. Look at your father.' She pointed in his direction and I looked over to him.

He was on a stepladder putting a net around the fig tree. The net was supposed to protect it from flying foxes. They came when the tree was fruiting and gobbled up the figs before we could pick them. Baba was wearing blue cargo shorts, a singlet and aviator sunglasses.

'He has been doing that all morning. Just invents things for himself to do.' She let out a sigh that came from her stomach, fell out of her, landed on the ground somewhere near her slippers.

The net around the fig tree actually did work. One night we were woken by a series of shrieks and clicks. We all put on our robes and went outside. Baba carried a torch. When he shone it at the tree, we saw a bat struggling in the net, tangling itself more and more. It made noises that were like muffled screams.

Baba handed me the torch. 'Keep your eyes on it,' he said.

'Where are you going?' I asked, but he didn't reply. I heard his feet stomping away across the grass.

'Probably doing something useless,' said Mama.

I pointed the torch at the bat. It stopped making noise. I took a few steps towards it and Mama tried to hold me back. 'Rabies!' Went closer and closer to it. The body had golden brown fur and it had a grey face that fell somewhere between terrifying and adorable. Moist round eyes that would blink hard, almost looked like tears welling up in black pools. Scary. But up close it was just scared.

'Move, Lambros.' I turned around. Baba was carrying a broom. Held it by the handle, made a large arc, swiping down on the bat in the net. The animal cried out. Fell to the lower parts of the net. Baba hit it again and again and again. It fell out of the net and onto the dirt underneath the tree. I was still shining the torch on it. The animal pushed out its arm. Raised its grey head to the sky, like it was looking for its maker. My dad prodded it with the broom. Then he started calling: 'Psst Psst. Psst Psst.'

The cat came and circled around the animal. It crouched, staring at the bat. It extended a paw slowly and tapped it twice. The bat turned its head towards Psst Psst and the cat wrapped its mouth around its neck, biting down hard, and the cat we recognised – cute thing that sat on Mama's lap – became mechanical, devoid of emotion. The three of us stood watching in silence as our cat killed the most Australian thing to fly into our yard.

By that time morning dew was already starting to form on the grass. The air was flirting with the cold, waiting for the sun to wake up and spread that sheet of subtropical weather over Sydney.

'Dry out the carcass and keep the bones,' Mama said to Baba.

He wrestled the bat off the cat and I went to bed.

The carcass was put on a metal tray in the corner of our yard. When the flesh had gone, Mama gave the bones a wash in the laundry. She sewed them into a Greek icon and then took the icon to the church up the road. Placed it in the foyer for the forty-day period required for them to be blessed.

'Bat bones are lucky,' said Mama. 'Bat bones are lucky on our island, but you can't kill a bat – that's unlucky.'

'But didn't Baba kill that bat?' I asked.

'It was the cat,' she retorted.

'But we own the cat,' I said.

She looked at me like she was fed up. 'No one owns a cat. Cats own people.'

Mama wrapped the bones up in material, put them under my bed. They stayed under my bed throughout my teenage years, well into my twenties. Didn't help nothing. Didn't stop my depressions. Didn't stop my psychosis. But I was still alive.

When I was all alone, I had this recurring dream. I was walking the streets of Birrong. Neat front yards were being fondled and gardened by hi-vis hotties that looked at me like a sidepiece. Pavement painted watercolour grey. Bushes and shrubs were like chess pieces. One guy in a yellow singlet stood on the nature strip. His shorts ended way above the knee and showed thick brown man thighs. He rammed the chainsaw harder into the banksia as he saw me approach. It ripped and whirled into my head and I was in such distress that I called my mama. Instead of Mama, there was a voice on the other end of the phone telling me things about myself that only I knew, like the fake names I gave at Gloria Jean's. As I kept walking, on the other side of the street I saw two pit bulls tethered to a line attached to an electricity pole. Just as the dogs ran at me, I woke up breathing shallow and rubbing my forehead. Outside I heard the neighbours pruning the trees and then I called my mama, for real this time.

Didn't like Mama's voice when she answered the phone. Hello was said like a sigh. Then she told me that there was another flock of black cockatoos in the macadamia tree. I read it as a sign. There was this disappointment in her voice, which accused me of not caring. That whole phone call was off. Rotten egg spoiled. Anyway, I wasn't on the Syrinapx and the earth was off its axis; perhaps

Atlas was shrugging. So before I started my late shift I went and saw her.

Took the train to Belmore and remembered why I bought a car. I sat in the top part of an empty carriage, turned the seats to face the direction that I was coming from. Someone had tried to tag the train recently – the anti-graf task squad cleaners had got to it, but they hadn't been able to get the ink completely off. Foot-long smudges where names had been resembled abstract watercolours, more beautiful than what either tagger or cleaner intended. Swirls where some poor Harry Hazara had tried to scrub off as much of the name as he could.

More and more people got on the train. But they went downstairs or stayed near the doors. As I passed through Bankstown I looked at the platforms full of people all staring into their phones. Teen hijabis who were more like valley girls updated their Snapchat. A recent reffo wearing brown pants and white leather brogues, checking Facebook. A black dad and white mama wearing matching Adidas tracksuits gripped a blue stroller in which a tiny boy sat looking at an iPhone with a broken screen. Under the billboards opposite the station were groups of cats. Cats in clusters sunning themselves. Single cats chasing lizards. Kittens doing that play pouncing, learning how to attack.

I remembered a theory I'd had as a kid. If I was taking the train towards the city from Belmore, moving closer and closer to the centre, I knew that I was moving in the right direction. But if I was heading west, towards Bankstown and Liverpool, I knew that my life was getting worse.

I got off the train at Belmore. Walked up the steps. Took the quickest route home. Hooked a right at the Art Deco toilet block that used to be a beat. Boarded-up now. Had to walk down a back street that I used to hate as a kid. It was one of those lanes that ran behind the main shops. It was a shitty in-between place that was full of rubbish and massive trucks trying to make deliveries in a too-small space. When I was a kid I'd always avoided the lane. Some friends had been mugged there. It was a place where deals went down. Junkies usually loitered. But then someone took down the official council street sign that said Redman Lane and put up a handmade sign that renamed it Sesame Street. After that, despite the overfilled dumpsters and the syringes in the gutters, the place didn't seem that bad.

When I got home Baba wasn't there. Used my old key and went into the house. Straight to Mama's bedroom, leaned on the doorframe, saw her lying in the bed, head raised by three pillows. Crammed into the room were a few old closets and two mattresses on their sides. Mama was heavy breathing, long slow sighs that shook the mattress. There was a smell of bile in the air.

'Why is all this furniture here?' I asked her.

'The Salvation Army gave it to us.'

'That doesn't answer anything,' I said.

'Hello to you.' She cracked a smile and then started coughing. I went and sat next to her on the bed.

'How you feeling today?' I asked and put my hand on her forehead. She was hot. Skin moist.

'I haven't eaten anything today because I wasn't hungry.'

'Nothing?' I said to her, the woman who empties the fridge before midday.

'I had three Vita-Weats. But I threw them all up.' She pointed to a red bucket next to the bed. There was a shallow pool of spew in it.

'My leg hurts,' she said.

Her left foot had a black tinge to the toes. The discolouration spread to the bottom of the sole. A couple of the nails were black.

She was wearing this nightgown made of white flannel with roses printed on it. I raised it above her ankle. Her leg was red and plump with the texture of boiled chicken. Prodded it a bit. Her mouth fought hard to hide the pain and present a smile. I sat with her in the dark and held her hand.

'It's been getting darker and darker for a while now,' she said.

I went around the house fetching boxes of tissues. Stocking up on some supplies she'd need when I was gone. In my old bedroom, I lifted up the mattress and found the parcel of material with bat bones inside. Put them under her bed. Spent some time moistening towels and putting them on her head. Changing them, getting new ones. After about five minutes the cool towel became warm. Both of us were silent.

'Listen, Mama,' I said. She opened her eyes. Looked at me but didn't move her head.

'I am gonna go to work now but I'll call later to check up on you.'

She nodded at me and rolled over to her side. I got up, walked to the door. She called me back, so I went and sat on the bed. She curled her index finger at me. Wanted me to come closer. Leaned over, but that wasn't close enough. She grabbed me by my chin and angled my ear towards her mouth. Opened her mouth, wind forming at her lips.

'I need to tell you this . . .' she said.

'Tι?' I asked her.

'Your face looks very young today. But your body lets you down.' She let go of my chin and I wiped my ear. As

I stood up she was already falling asleep. I left quickly, scared Baba would be back any minute.

I walked down Lakemba Street. On one of the low brick walls there were three old Greek women sitting together, watching the cars go past. I raised my hand at them and yelled, 'Yia sas,' and they greeted me in return. I recognised one of them as Mina, who I'd seen in Dr Athena's surgery. She just raised her arm – a slight wave. Didn't ask me about anything. Didn't stop me to chat.

I let my head drop. Looked at the pavement. Weeds growing through cracks.

Maybe it was remembering all those Greeks in the surgery waiting room. Looking at me and asking how one of their own went so bad. Maybe it was remembering the way Telly was spotting Nice Arms Pete in the gym while I spied on them, then getting that feeling of outrage and arousal. Maybe it was dreaming about the two dogs tethered to an electricity pole and waking up with a sense of dread. I hooked up one of the side streets and found myself dead in front of Telly's house. All the trees around it jiggled in the heat. Next to the house a woman in activewear carefully opened her gate, looked up and down the street, carefully walked out.

'Watch out for his dogs,' she said to me as she rushed to her hybrid.

Looked back at the house. Still had the chain-link fence. The gate creaked when I opened it. I walked up the path. Knocked on the door. Looked at the six-foot-high wooden gate next to the house, timber colour reddish blond, hadn't turned grey – yet. Little gap beneath the gate: two sets of paws. I rang the doorbell but no one answered. Cars went down the street, wind blew over red-tiled rooftops. I stood on the path, the tips of my fingers sparkling. Base of spine pulsing. Syrinapx part of my system. Underneath the skin on my cheeks, little earthquakes shook hidden nerves. Felt my face being torn apart. Pulled the phone out of my pocket and checked the time. Saw dog paws move through the space under the gate. They paced up and down, stalking the entrance. I flipped on my heel and made a quick getaway to work.

PARK ROAD

Took the bus to work. I hunched over my phone, scrolled through the photos. Pictures of Nice Arms Pete asleep, pictures of his arse popping out of the bed, a muscled arm extended on a pillow. Pictures of The Doc asleep, his head turned, facing away from me. White neck and brown, fresh cut hair, looking like a stock image that someone would use to illustrate an article about sleeping pills.

Focus was hard for me. The lights of the streetlamps turned into pale blue pills. Hubcaps of cars passing the bus looked like the lids of Syrinapx bottles. Thought that I should have pocketed some when I was at Mama's but was too stressed at the time.

When I got to work I looked at the shifts roster. The Doc's name had an annual leave mark next to it. Sent him an SMS, wondering when I would see him again. He didn't reply immediately and I got that craving for Syrinapx. Head thick. Mind jumping from The Doc to my job. Breathed into it. Felt my forehead on permanent crease.

Got my trolley, cleaning products and sheets. Started the rounds.

Bruno seemed more agitated than usual. Eyes constantly looked around. His legs were dead weights. He pulled the thin sheet up to his neck, rolled it down then pulled it up again.

'How are you doing this morning?' I asked.

'It's the afternoon,' Bruno corrected me, summoning a smile.

I held down my need to see The Doc. That need to see him, mixed into the painkiller want. Checked my phone; no reply from him.

'I just knew he would come back,' Bruno said. He looked out the window, at the sun descending behind an aluminium fence. 'It's Peter. He came back to me. His hair was golden too.'

I stopped wiping the nightstand, turned back to Bruno.

The ones that get dementia? Forget about it. From happy to sad in a second. Their worst fears spew out. Dementia means that people are no longer people. Minds are fizzled. Bruno's eyes were shaky. I could feel myself separating from the Bruno that I loved. Hard, because I saw myself in him. I could have been Bruno if I was born in a different generation. I could have loved someone and then they disappeared. I made my mind race to the future. Would I be bed-bound as some young man cleaned around me?

'Peter?' I repeated. 'From your old life? From the photo next to your bed?' I looked at the tall white guy standing next to Bruno on the beach.

Bruno nodded. His eyes were wide and glassy. The gestures of a child from a scruffy grey-haired old man.

'I've seen him too,' said Pasquale from the next bed. His eyes were milky with cataracts and stared blankly into the distance. He put in his dentures and started to talk. 'Well, I heard him. He comes in with a bunch of ruffling papers, says hello to all of us . . . he has a deep voice.'

'Papers?' I asked.

'Yes, him and his brother – with papers,' said Pasquale.

'Brother?' My voice went up at the end.

'Yes! Papers and brother!'

My right hand dropped the Chux I was wiping with. My left hand dropped the antibacterial spray gun to the floor. It spilled yellow liquid over blue-speckled linoleum.

'Bruno?' I said.

He looked up at me.

'Is it just them? Just the brothers?'

Bruno sighed and didn't answer. Felt my chest closing in. Quick breaths, too short. I walked to reception. Uneven steps. Little skips to move more quickly.

At the reception desk I flipped through the pages of the visitors book. Back a few days. My finger went down the list of residents' names, found an entry marked *Bruno*. Next to it was a name, Peter Kelly: Nice Arms Pete. Visited at 10 am on a Monday. Turned the pages for the next few days. Looked at all the guests for Tuesday – no one for Bruno. On Wednesday found Peter Kelly's name next to Bruno again. And on the Thursday a visit from Peter Kelly and a Mr William Sexton. My veins, a pulsating river running across my forehead to my temples; the blood pooled in corners and throbbed.

I looked around for the receptionist. Saw the clock on the wall, realised she had left for the day. Took the book and tried to walk off with it, but it was tied to the desk. Put the book back and stood there. Noticed the room around me. The walls were cheap, pale blue and where they met the ceiling they were starting to crack.

I went and sat on the bench in the staffroom. Checked my phone to see if there were any messages from The Doc. None.

There were connections, clues, all over the place now that I saw it in a different light.

Thought I'd seen Nice Arms Pete hooking up with Trainer Bob at Maluga Passive Park and had walked away, not wanting to see hands go in and out of pants and mouths around dicks. Looking back, they'd probably sat down, swapped numbers and recognised something in each other.

Thought that Nice Arms Pete listened to the stories I told about Bruno because he liked migrant homo stories. Realised now he was gleaning info.

Thought that I was the only staff member Trainer Bob did the one-on-one training with. But maybe The Doc had met him too or maybe they knew each other from the gay world. Maybe this was brewing before I came to work at the home.

Thought that Rushcutters Bay was a place for photos, where Telly and Nice Arms Pete could wear Australian flag Speedos and pose. But my imagination had only extended to flirting between William Sexton and Nice Arms Pete. What I didn't picture was The Doc in the corner, watching it all unravel, listening to the click, click, click of the camera.

Thought that the toothy blow job I gave to The Doc at work was an expression of something, but really I was just a plot device, a convenient happenstance, something they could use. And there I was, the perfect patsy, the fall guy, the link and the distraction from the real crime.

'Bucky, are you okay?'

I raised my head. Agatha was unzipping her uniform. I nodded and watched her remove her yoyo and swipe and put it on the bench. She took a mobile phone out of her front pocket and put it down next to the swipe.

'Have you finished your PM duties?' she asked.

I shrugged, my eyes darting to the yoyo and then back to her. 'Seems that Bruno's dementia is in full swing,' I said.

'Have you finished your PM duties?' she repeated.

Went to give an excuse but her phone rang. She held up one finger to me and took the call, speaking in Tagalog. She went into the change room. Heard her talking, muted through the door. I picked up her yoyo, swiped the e-lock and entered the room full of drugs. Four plastic bottles of Syrinapx went in my left pocket. Another four went in my right pocket. Put two in my back pocket and exited the drug cave. Went straight to my locker to hide the goodies. Agatha kept talking away in the bathroom. Was closing the locker door when Agatha came out. I was still holding her yoyo and swipe in my hand. I curled my fingers around them, hiding them from her.

'Sorry, that was a personal call I had to take,' she said.

'I'm just having a cigarette break,' I said. Put my hands in the pockets of my pants, slouched into the blue scrubs.

'One of the cleaners wanted to see you.' Something to redirect her. Trying to get her out of the room. As she walked towards the door, I dropped the swipe on the floor close to her desk.

'Make sure you get the meals out on time tonight,' said Agatha.

In the courtyard, I smoked a cigarette. The temporary relief this brought was overwhelmed by anger. I dialled The Doc. The phone rang out. I dialled Nice Arms Pete and the phone rang and rang in my eardrum. I called my mama. She answered on the sixth ring. She still hadn't eaten anything. She was still throwing up. She still felt dizzy and then she dropped the phone. Heard a thud. Heard a crash. I yelled out her name. *Thea! Thea! Thea!* Decided to ditch work and go to Mama.

CECILIA STREET

In the car, going to see Mama. Popped two blue moons on the way there. Turned off the radio because my AM wasn't working. Didn't want to hear the FM stations and their shows called 'Bit and Drongo's Arvo Cuppa i-Mix Hour'. Didn't want to hear songs that I would love in the moment and forget about in a month. Was going down Lakemba Street when I got a phone call from work. Put the call on speaker.

'Lambros, where did you go?' It was Agatha.

'My mama is sick. I have to take her to the hospital.'

'I don't know if that's true.' Her voice filled the car; it was like she was all around me.

'She is. Swear she is.'

'We are having some problems here. I think you need to come in right now.' There was a schoolteacher tone in her voice.

I knew what she was talking about but pretended I didn't. 'Sorry about the residents' meals. I really had to take care of my ma.'

'There are medications missing from the meds closet.'

'I don't have access to that closet,' I said.

'I called around. Dr Martin said you might have taken his swipe. I am very sorry, but I am going to have to call the police.'

'I can't talk now. I have to see my mama.' I ended the call as I pulled into the driveway. Baba was sitting in an armchair by the window. He looked at me then turned his head away.

I ran up the front steps, opened the door and went straight into Mama's bedroom.

She hadn't moved since I'd left her. Her face and legs were on fire. Tried talking to her. She kept going in and out of consciousness. She turned to look at me and I tried looking for the memories I knew were in her eyes. There was no woman working at the library. There was no teen washing her clothes in a mountain stream, using ash to remove stains.

Called the emergency line. Told them what the deal was. They put me through to a registered nurse and I repeated her symptoms, repeated her symptoms, repeated her symptoms. They said they would send an ambulance to take her to Canterbury Hospital.

I sat on Mama's bed. Put moist face washers on her forehead. Sometimes she looked through me. Sometimes she couldn't keep her eyes open. Sometimes she looked up at me and said, 'You are my city.' The sun went down. I looked out the bedroom window and saw red and blue flashing lights light up the citrus trees. Mandarins and lemons glowed like blue-red baubles. The ambulance pulled into our driveway. Sound was off. Lights were flashing. No drama of the Waaah! Waaah! Waaah! sound but flashing lights drew the neighbours out. Took three paramedics fifteen minutes to get her out of bed. They put Mama onto a stretcher. Wheeled her out. People had come from down the road to look on.

Out the front, I looked for Nice Arms Pete, The Doc or Telly. But what I saw was worse. Just the neighbours. People with nice families and grandparents. People who had Christmases full of toddlers and happy relatives. People who had heard our screaming matches, who had fights with us about bins and dumping rubbish on the kerb and knew that we had an old weird car.

I noticed a cop car there. Two uniforms and a man in a suit got out. One of the cops walked towards me. Said my name. Turned around, saw my dad sitting in his armchair looking out the window. One hand holding the curtain open. A slight catch in his eyebrows. A slight catch that said *I told you so.*

Flashing lights lit up the street. The colour red panned across fences and front gates. The colour red on metal letterboxes. The colour red on banksia trees that grew just under the power lines. The colour red streamed down to the end of our street, across a hazard sign that had black-and-white diagonal stripes and the cop said my name, took slow steps towards me, and the neighbours were looking on and the cop said my name and I—

I get up before the sun does. Think that I hear steps of an ex around the house but it's just the guards doing their rounds. I lie on my back; the hard bed straightens my spine. The room is temperature-controlled, no sheets necessary. Morning sequence is pending and I say to the air in the cell, 'You know what?' in that deep Greek intonation that goes up at the end. My mind jumps, races and skids – bald tyres on a slick road. 'Nice Arms Pete and The Doc, they come from the same place.' Concrete walls don't have an answer, so I'm another crazy. Another one of the forty-nine percent of the Australian prison population with a mental health problem. But sometimes I think I'm not. Sometimes I think I'm a Greek living under the taxes of the Ottoman pasha. Or I am an Athenian under the rule of the junta. Really I'm another one, under the time policing of a warden. So I go back to symbols. Try to read the signs. Remake them into myths, interpret cheap objects and dreams.

As I look up at the ceiling, I see my name coming at me. Because really. At the start of this. All of this. Is my name. Lambraki, Baki, Bucky, Bux. They are all me.

To be fair I was Mama Theodesia's connection to this place. But were we citizens in the city? Or land-owning peasants in the village? We still read currawongs as friends of catastrophe while we sipped on VB shandies. We still put the bat bones under our mattresses and wished for some good hocus pocus while plonking ourselves in front of static-filled TV screens. We still foraged the nature strips in search of wild weeds. My baba – he was King of his Country with a Faggot for a Son. My baba swapped me for the native and introduced pigeons that sat on his fences and driveway. They waited for his plastic bag full of seed feed in the morning. Cresty pigeon and its brood. One-legged bird with speckled wings. Those were really his children, not me.

And for a while there, during those brief periods of sitting on chairs, handcuffed and waiting for my Legal Aid solicitor, I would pause, imagine that Nice Arms Pete and The Doc were the same person. But I realised they

weren't. So I said, 'Demons – demons made me do it!'
And people thought I believed in a devil with horns and
an arrow tail. Local newspapers made their subeditors'
jobs easy with a headline that read: GAY STEALS FROM
MEDS CLOSET, DEVILS MADE HIM DO IT! What I meant
were the blue-eyed demons, with their pink nips. Those
demons have radio-frequency connections to Australian
flags as capes, flecks of beach sand on the Southern Cross.
But my mind was set like the tar they pour into the
potholes. Syrinapx. Those little blue moons that had a
gravity so strong they kept me in a blind orbit.

When I was in court, words came out of the stand,
testifying against me – I turned my head back, covered
my neck with my hand. I saw Nice Arms Pete all Guy
Incognito – Tarocash summer sale fashion, sitting in the
back row – whispering into the ear of William Sexton.
I squinted at them and the breath ran from my body.

Never saw Telly again. There went the wogs. Telly
and me could have been twins. Instead we fought for the
same piece of land, which presented itself as the country
of the mind but was really just someone else's rundown
playground and all the kids had been kicked out. Still
craved the two blue moons. Syrinapx puffed through the
air. It was smoke now. Gone boy!

Lying in bed, I twist my neck to see the wall. I'm in
the mountain village ancestral home, a library print of it

stuck on the wall via sugar and saliva. I can see Mama's old primary school, the one wall that's left of it. There are some firs and conifers all around. She's not dead yet and I call her from the payphone reverse charges. I smoke cigarettes here. When I drop them they burn holes in my clothes and soul. But the art therapy classes keep me charged. I have reimagined the bat under the fig tree in pictures. It's still reaching up to God as it dies but the cat killing it – sucking out the air from its throat – has the biceps of Nice Arms Pete, the hook nose of my father and The Doc's rimless glasses.

Street names are all up on the wall in a collage now. These streets, right here, they my real home. Maps printed, road names and parks circled with a contraband Sharpie. Haldon Street is nothing without my low-budget coming-of-age sex movie memories and subsequent stalking. Auburn Road – wiped from my cortex. Cecilia Street. Burwood Road. Lakemba Street. They have their columned houses, vegie gardens and ζαχοραπλαστεια. Those things and the churches aren't just in the signs; they are in my mitochondria.

Part of me says fuck it. Let 'em have those physical spaces.

Who cares if an old πούστι with dementia and milk-eye cataracts gets swindled out of his houses? They are just weeds growing out of a window, they are just a dirty old park with a boarded-up toilet block. Canyons of flats and abandoned rental homes can't speak to you about the doubles of my life and the circular family that wrapped themselves around me.

You really wanna know what?

Those streets are a map to how I ended up here. Follow them on my wall. Put your finger on the place where I got bashed, fucked, addicted and became a dickhead. The Hume is just another one of those arterials. That's all.

ACKNOWLEDGEMENTS

This started in a carpark at night. Someone pointed at me and asked a smart-ass hack 'What are we gonna do with him?'. The smart-ass hack didn't miss a beat. 'Make him do genre . . . but which kind?'

I fingered my mother of pearl cigarette case. A curl of hair fell across my forehead. 'What if I did Noir . . . baby,' I said as I lit my cigarette.

The smart-ass hack was David Henley of *Seizure*. Him and his partner, Alice Grundy, were involved in a collaboration with SWEATSHOP to make an anthology called *Stories of Sydney*. I workshopped a short story called *More Handsome Than a Monkey* in our writing collective and couldn't let go of the voice.

If I recall correctly – which I'm sure I don't – it seemed to be around this time that me, Michael Mohammed Ahmad and Luke Carman were developing the show #Three Jerks. We did a reading at Sydney Writers' Festival and Sam Twyford-Moore championed us at the Emerging Writers' Festival in Melbourne.

After the show in Melbourne two things happened. Robert Watkins from Hachette approached me. Eventually I learned that his floral-print bow ties and polka dots were just a distraction from the formidable person underneath. The other thing that stuck was Maxine Beneba Clarke's review of #Three Jerks, which says that this country's stories are 'heading for the Hume'. *Down the Hume* was born.

I did coffee with Robert and realised behind his anglerfish-lure clothing was someone that was smart and hard. I pitched him the idea. He looked at me with a raised eyebrow. I sent Robert some chapters and then I was the one raising an eyebrow when he said he was interested.

I kept workshopping *Down the Hume* in the SWEATSHOP writers collective but the dirty work left me hard up for cash. I applied to WestWords for some moula and mentoring through the CAL Western Sydney Writers' Fellowship. I got blessed with Dr Sara Knox.

Sara Knox, AKA The School of Hard Knox, was exactly what the dippy fag in me needed. She did more work than she needed to, and without her input I'd still be wandering the queer desert.

Something was missing though. This character lived in a female-less world, and it was about this time that Rosie Dennis commissioned work for me for Urban Theatre Projects. The work I did for Rosie unstitched my heart and ebbed and flowed into this book.

This paper baby is done because of the people above.

This paper baby will show everyone the worst aspects of me. Obsession. Addiction. Paranoia. But during this process, I have relied on the best aspects of the people around me. Robert and Mo especially.

Peter Polites is a writer of Greek descent from Western Sydney. As part of the SWEATSHOP writers collective, Peter has written and performed pieces all over Australia. Alongside *Sydney Morning Herald* Best Young Australian Novelists Luke Carman and Michael Mohammed Ahmad, Polites wrote and performed #Three Jerks – a spoken-word piece about the Cronulla riots – to sellout crowds in Sydney and Melbourne. He has recently been commissioned to write a play about the migrant experience in Western Sydney for the Sydney Festival, to be performed in 2017. *Down the Hume* is his first novel.

hachette
AUSTRALIA

If you would like to find out more about Hachette Australia,
our authors, upcoming events and new releases you can visit
our website, Facebook or follow us on Twitter:

hachette.com.au
facebook.com/HachetteAustralia
twitter.com/HachetteAus